Angel

Hugo von Hofmannsthal
SELECTED TALES

HUGO VON HOFMANNSTHAL was born in Vienna on 1 February 1874 into a patrician family of Austrian, Jewish, Bavarian and Italian stock. Still at school, he won acclaim with his early poems which, like his short lyric dramas *Yesterday* (1891) and *Death and the Fool* (1893), brilliantly capture the decadent spirit of the *fin de siècle*. In 1892 he began to study law at Vienna University, but after a year's military service with the Sixth Dragoons (1893-4) switched to Romance Languages with a view to an academic career. In his twenties he published literary essays and his most intriguing and avant-garde short prose works, *The Tale of the 672nd Night* (1895), *A Cavalry Tale* (1899), *Marshal de Bassompierre's Adventure* (1900) and *Letter from Lord Chandos* (1902).

In 1901 he married Gertrude Schlesinger from a banking family and settled in a Baroque villa in the Vienna suburb of Rodaun to pursue a career as an independent man of letters. Over the next three decades he wrote numerous plays, including adaptations of Sophocles' *Electra* (1903), *Oedipus the King* (1910) and the English morality play *Everyman* (1911), and two outstanding social comedies, *The Difficult Man* (1921) and *The Incorruptible* (1923). In his long collaboration with Richard Strauss he wrote the libretti for *Der Rosenkavalier* (1911), *Ariadne on Naxos* (1912), *The Woman without a Shadow* (1913) and *Arabella* (1929), the last two adapted from his own prose pieces. His work with the producer Max Reinhardt in establishing the Salzburg Festival and his long philosophical drama *The Tower* (begun in 1925) contributed to Austria's cultural regeneration after 1914–18. Hofmannsthal died of a stroke on 15 July 1929. He is buried in the Kalkstein Cemetery in Vienna.

J. M. Q. DAVIES read German and Modern Greek at Oxford and spent two years in Vienna before pursuing an academic career in English and Comparative Literature. Among his translations from German are three volumes of short fiction and plays by Arthur Schnitzler.

Arthur Schnitzler translated by J. M. Q. Davies

Selected Short Fiction
Dream Story
Round Dance and other Plays

HUGO von HOFMANNSTHAL

Selected Tales

The Tale of the 672nd Night
A Cavalry Tale
Marshal de Bassompierre's Adventure
Letter from Lord Chandos
and other narratives

Translated with an introduction and notes by
J. M. Q. DAVIES

ANGEL BOOKS
London

First published in 2007 by
Angel Books, 3 Kelross Road, London N5 2QS
1 3 5 7 9 10 8 6 4 2

A CIP catalogue record for this book is available from the British Library

ISBN-13: 978-0-946162-74-1
ISBN-10: 0-946162-74-3

This book is printed on acid free paper conforming to the British library
recommendations and to the full American standard

Acknowledgement is made to the Arts Division of the
Austrian Federal Chancellery for financial assistance
towards meeting the cost of translation

Typeset in 10½ on 12½ pt Monotype Ehrhardt by
Ray Perry, Woodstock, Oxon.
Printed and bound in Great Britain by Biddles Ltd,
King's Lynn, Norfolk

Contents

Introduction

THERE IS AN abiding fascination to turn-of-the-century Vienna, that brief interlude, so brutally cut short by the Great War, when the staid Danubian capital once again became a major centre of artistic innovation and home or host to a galaxy of early Modernist talent – Klimt, Schiele and the other Secessionists; Schnitzler, Bahr, Hofmannsthal and their fellow 'Young Vienna' writers; Freud, Mach, Mahler, Richard Strauss and Schönberg. Less well known internationally today (except as Strauss's librettist) and temperamentally the antithesis of his older friend and rival, the philandering Arthur Schnitzler, Hugo von Hofmannsthal (1874–1929) was a man of immense idealism and intellectual ambition, who devoted his life to enriching the cultural heritage of his beloved Austria in any way that opportunity allowed. Schnitzler, like Chekhov, trained as a physician; his plays and fiction exploring the erotic obsessions and rising anti-semitism of the times always gravitate towards the naturalistic, even when formally innovative. Hofmannsthal, a more visionary writer, an accomplished linguist and a man of letters to his fingertips, experimented with a much wider range of traditional forms, in most of which he made rich use of symbolism – lyric poems, oriental fairytales, classical and medieval dramas, social comedies, short fiction, ballet and opera libretti, travel sketches, aphorisms, essays. Within these conventions he contrived to produce a handful of outstanding works which today strike one as extraordinarily modern and disturbing. This is particularly true of the stories translated in the present selection, in which a young aesthete's psychic crack-up, a cavalry sergeant's insubordination, the enigmatic motives of a *femme fatale,* or the agony of a writer's block transcend their very varied period settings and, like Kafka's parabolic tales, achieve a quasi-archetypal status and linger on in the mind.

Hofmannsthal's international reputation has undoubtedly, however, been tarnished by political aspersions and the ironies of history.[1] With his profound interest in Europe's cultural heritage, he was more politically thoughtful than many writers who matured during the halcyon years before the First World War, Rainer Maria Rilke or Hermann Hesse, for instance, or the early Thomas Mann. Yet he too was innocent of *Realpolitik* and in retrospect his wartime essays advocating a revitalised Europe under Habsburg leadership seem curiously quixotic. By 1945, even though he had died in 1929 before Hitler came to power, he was being associated by left-wing intellectuals with Nazism, and his idealistic late Romantic enthusiasm for an organic multi-ethnic society, with roots in folk culture, was being miscon-strued as proto-Fascist. But today it is widely acknowledged that this brilliant, diffident, 'seismographically' sensitive and at times mystical writer, who identified with Keats's 'chameleon' poet quick to empathise with others and felt drawn to Eastern cultures, was essentially a conciliatory spirit for whom art was a way of understanding and harmonising the tensions and div-isions of the modern world. In many ways he was a tragic figure. As the old tolerant inefficient Habsburg order fell apart, he became increasingly conscious of being – like Franz Grillparzer, Austria's national poet, before him – a prophet out of step with his times. He once poignantly remarked that though at the height of his creative powers he was not receiving any commissions. And when he died of a stroke only days after his son's suicide, many saw it as an omen. But a century on, his imaginative evoca-tions of epiphanic, near-death or quasi-schizoid states, his aware-

---

[1] A full account of the fluctuations in Hofmannsthal's reputation is provided by Douglas A. Joyce, 'Hofmannsthal Reception in the Twentieth Century' in *A Companion to the Works of Hugo von Hofmannsthal*, edited by Thomas A. Kovach (New York: Camden House, 2002), pages 227–50 and by Kovach's introduction to that volume, pages 1–22.

ness of the gulf between language and experience, his quest for authentic values in a world of transience, his suspicion of material progress divorced from any sense of history and his idealistic vision of a European community don't seem so irrelevant.

An amusing summary of the cultural changes sweeping turn-of-the-century Vienna is provided by Robert Musil in *The Man without Qualities* (1930–43):

> The just-buried century in Austria could not be said to have covered itself with glory during its second half. It had been clever in technology, business and science, but beyond these focal points of its energy it was stagnant and treacherous as a swamp. It had painted like the Old Masters, written like Goethe and Schiller, and built its houses in the style of the Gothic and the Renaissance. The demands of the ideal ruled like a police headquarters over all expressions of life ... and – relevant or not – the women of the period, who were as chaste as they were shy, had to wear dresses that covered them from the ears down to the ground while showing off a billowing bosom and a voluptuous behind ... Suddenly, out of the becalming mentality of the nineteenth century's last two decades, an invigorating fever rose all over Europe. No one knew exactly what was in the making; nobody could have said whether it was to be a new art, a new humanity, a new morality, or perhaps a reshuffling of society. So everyone said what he pleased about it. But everywhere people were suddenly standing up to struggle against the old order ... There were those who loved the overman and those who loved the underman; there were health cults and sun cults and cults of consumptive maidens; there was enthusiasm for the hero worshippers and for the believers in the Common Man; people were devout and sceptical, naturalistic and mannered, robust and morbid; they dreamed of old tree-lined avenues in palace parks, autumnal gardens, glassy ponds, gems, hashish, disease, and demonism, but also of prairies, immense horizons, forges and rolling mills, naked wrestlers, slave uprisings, early man, and the smashing of society.[2]

---

[2] Robert Musil, *The Man without Qualities*, translated by Sophie Wilkins (London: Picador, 1995), pages 52–54. A rich source of further background information on many of the topics touched on by Musil in this passage is Carl E. Schorske, *Fin-de-siècle Vienna: Politics and Culture* (New York: Random House, 1961).

This might almost be a mirror of the divisions within Hofmannsthal's own soul – deeply wedded to Austria's cultural legacy yet very much part of this invigorating modernist fever. Cosmopolitan by birth as well as disposition and linguistic training, he was the only son in a family of mixed Austrian, Jewish, Italian and Bavarian origins. His great-grandfather, a successful silk merchant, had been elevated to the lesser nobility, but the family fortune he founded was reduced by the stock-market crash of 1873. During his sheltered childhood Hofmannsthal was especially close to his maternal grandmother, who would speak Italian to him and take him to the Burgtheater, kindling his lifelong enthusiasm for the magic of the theatre and for actors and dancers like Friedrich Mitterwurzer, Eleonora Duse and Isadora Duncan. Between 1884 and 1892 he attended the prestigious neo-gothic Academic Gymnasium where he received a classical humanist education, excelling in all subjects except science. To oblige his provident banker father he then embarked on a law course at Vienna University, while also frequenting the cultivated Döbling salons of the elderly Josephine von Wertheimstein (1820–94) – a meeting-place for liberal politicians, artists and writers. (The mutual attachment between poet and hostess would form the nucleus for the more idealised relationship between the seventeen-year-old Octavian and the thirty-two-year-old Marschallin in *Der Rosenkavalier*, 1911.) His studies were interrupted by twelve months (1894–95) of military service with the Sixth Dragoons in the bleak town of Göding near the Czech border, which though at times emotionally depressing he recognised as character-building and would later talk about with pride. On his return to Vienna he switched to a combined course in art history and Romance philology and literature, submitting a linguistic study of the *Pléiade* poets in 1897 and a higher doctoral thesis – necessary for an academic career – on Victor Hugo in 1901. When it looked as though extensive revisions to the latter might be required, however, he withdrew pleading a nervous indisposition and severed his formal ties with the university. The same year he married Gertrude Schlesinger, daughter of the Secretary-General of the Anglo-Austrian Bank, and settled in the suburb of Rodaun in a small villa dating from the reign of Maria Theresa, with Watteauesque panelling, a tiled stove and a summer house for writing. In this idyllic retreat from the 'reshuffling' and eventual 'smashing' of society, he led the life of the model English country gentleman he admired and would fictionalise in his *Letter from Lord Chandos* (1902), struggling to adapt the high-culture traditions of Goethe and Schiller to a modern vision of the world, holidaying in the Salzburg region and occasionally in Italy, Greece and Morocco, corresponding with and entertaining a widening circle of Europe's literati, including Gerhart Hauptmann, Max Reinhardt and the historian Carl J. Burckhardt.

Yet this is all merely the respectable Apollonian surface to the darker Dionysian shadow side of Hofmannsthal's complex, driven and astonishingly precocious creative personality. While still at school he had read extraordinarily widely, devouring everything from the great books of the Renaissance to 'robust' naturalists like Ibsen, 'demonists' like Baudelaire, and devotees of 'gems, hashish [and] disease' like Huysmans. By 1890, at the age of sixteen, he had begun to publish poems in the cultural sections of *Die Presse*, *Moderne Rundschau* and *Die Zeit* under the pseudonym of 'Loris'. And over the next three years he wrote a number of in some ways Yeatsean lyric dramas – notably *Yesterday* (*Gestern*, 1890) and *Death and the Fool* (*Der Tor und der Tod*, 1893*)* – which captured the mood of satiety and paralysis of the Austrian *fin de siècle*. In an essay on D'Annunzio (1893) he summed up his 'belated' generation's legacy from the age of Offenbach and Leopardi as 'pretty furniture and over-refined nerves'. And in *The Tale of the 672nd Night* (1895), perhaps his most powerful story, he portrayed the dangerous detachment from reality of an affluent representative of this generation – enjoying the fruits of his father's industry to decadent excess while lacking any function or categorical imperative in life.

Hofmannsthal's early publications quickly attracted the attention of the progressive Young Vienna circle of writers and intellectuals meeting in the Café Griensteidl, who welcomed him as a prodigy and the new voice of Symbolism (the term was sometimes used as a synonym for Decadence) in Vienna. Hermann Bahr recalled his shock when the mature writer he was expecting introduced himself in shorts, and Schnitzler, impressed by Hofmannsthal's readings and intellectual maturity, recorded that for the first time he had come face to face with authentic genius. The Berlin poet Stefan George, eager for contributions to his new aestheticist journal *Blätter für die Kunst*, sought him out in December 1891, hailing him as a 'twin brother' and presenting him with a manuscript copy of Mallarmé's *L'Après-midi d'un Faune* (1876). Indeed, so ardent was his courtship, sending flowers to the school, that Hofmannsthal asked his father to intervene and for a while a duel threatened. (In a posthumous tribute to his friend, Leopold von Andrian later declared that Hofmannsthal was unequivocally heterosexual but held male friendship in high esteem – a fact amply attested by his extensive correspondence.[3]) The episode certainly played a part in his characterisation of the merchant's son in *The Tale of the 672nd Night*, and nearly twenty years later in *Lucidor* (1910) he would explore the threshold between male and female, adolescence and maturity in the light-hearted comic spirit of *A Midsummer Night's Dream*. All this early recognition helped Hofmannsthal surmount his insecure sense of personal identity, his emotional detachment from others and the proneness to depression which plagued him all his life and, as with Virginia Woolf, was the obverse side of his hyperactive nature. He was also permanently influenced by Young Vienna's open, interdisciplinary spirit, unconstrained by academic specialisation. At the university he attended lectures by the sensationist psychologist Ernst Mach for instance, and later found many of his own intuitions endorsed in Morton Prince's study of schizophrenia, *The Dissociation of a Personality* (1905). His youthful essays on Bahr,

---

[3] Quoted in *Hugo von Hofmannsthal: Die Gestalt des Dichters im Spiegel der Freunde*, edited by Helmut A. Fiechtner (Vienna: Humboldt, 1949), page 62.

Barrès, Swinburne and D'Annunzio consider the rival claims of life and art in an impressive spectrum of intellectual contexts, from Goethe through Tolstoy to Pater, and pictorial techniques and parallels are almost a hallmark of his work in every genre.

Not surprisingly, by the time he was twenty-eight he felt burnt out. Looking back on this first so-called 'lyric' phase of his career, in which he had written what are regarded as some of the finest poems since Goethe, Hofmannsthal wryly remarked that if like his beloved Keats he had died young his reputation would have been secure. The extraordinary *Letter from Lord Chandos* written at this time, which transposes his personal sense of exhaustion into a more philosophic key – dramatising a Renaissance poet's crisis of faith in the expressive powers of language itself – marks a hiatus in his writing, after which he turned to the more public, less introverted medium of the theatre, with upward of twenty further plays, adaptations and libretti. For a writer with Hofmannsthal's rich sense of literary tradition, intertextuality and artifice, originality was quite as possible in modern adaptations of the Electra, Oedipus and Ariadne myths as in plays in the realistic mode of Schnitzler or Hauptmann. In *Electra* (1903; operatic version 1909), for instance, he combines quasi-Freudian insights into hysteria, echoes of Wilde's *Salome* (1893) and expressionistic dance techniques in a very *fin de siècle* portrait of woman as demonic.[4] Classical themes were also more likely to gain acceptance on the Vienna stage, less liberal than the theatre in Berlin. *The Woman without a Shadow (Die Frau ohne Schatten*, 1913; operatic version 1919) shows him experimenting in a quite different direction, that of allegorical prose fable. With its complicated plot and Blakean vision of redemption through union of body and spirit and sacrifice for others, it suffers from obscurity and clutter but hardly from lack of imaginative

---

[4] For a full discussion of this play in historical context see Hofmannsthal, *Selected Plays & Libretti*, edited and translated by Michael Hamburger et al. (London: Routledge, 1963), pages xxxif., where the distinction is made between 'Goethe's "humane" and Hofmannsthal's "barbaric" treatment of Greek myth'.

exuberance. Different again are the mystery plays *Everyman* (*Jedermann*, 1911) and *The Salzburg Great Theatre of the World* (*Das Salzburger grosser Welttheater*, 1922), which were deployed to rally a shell-shocked Austria and first produced by the anti-Naturalist director Max Reinhardt. The former in particular has an austere simplicity which was also part of Hofmannsthal's nature, and appears less archaic when construed as he intended in humanist rather than doctrinally Christian terms. Two of the creative highlights of his later career are *The Difficult Man* (*Der Schwierige*, 1921) and *The Incorruptible* (*Der Unbestechliche*, 1923), sophisticated social comedies, somewhat in the mode of Oscar Wilde and Henry James, in which feudal chivalric and modern materialist values are ironically counterpointed. And throughout his life Hofmannsthal continued to produce highly original and perceptive essays which collectively constitute a fascinating commentary both on their author and on his times, the topics ranging from the obsessiveness of Balzac's characters to differences between the Austrian and the Prussian temperament and the redemptive role of literature in the wake of the Great War.

Hofmannsthal's fiction – much of it left fragmentary as his work for the theatre took over – represents only a fraction of his total output, but it includes some of his most powerfully impressive achievements. Compared to that of older Austrian regionalists like Adalbert Stifter, Marie von Ebner-Eschenbach and Ferdinand von Saar, it strikes a distinctly modernist and cosmopolitan note, and anticipates the complex use of symbolism of Thomas Mann and Kafka. Like his mentor Hermann Bahr, Hofmannsthal felt that Naturalism was an artistic dead-end, and his fiction is a record of tireless innovation, ranging from brief impressionist sketches, somewhat in the manner of his Young Vienna associate Peter Altenberg, through travel pieces, dialogues celebrating the ecstasy of dance or hymns to the glorious colour of Van Gogh, to complex psychological allegories like the unfinished and posthumously published novel *Andreas, or the United* (*Andreas, oder die Vereinigten*, 1932). This experimental spirit is evident in the variety of literary antecedents, forms, settings and narrative techniques he uses in the present selection of short narratives, all but two of which were published initially in Vienna newspapers with a broadly middle-class readership. *Justice (Gerechtigkeit*, 1893) and *A Chance Glimpse of Happiness (Das Glück am Weg*, 1893) are short Symbolist prose poems. *The Tale of the 672nd Night (Das Märchen der 672. Nacht*, 1895) has the trappings of a high Romantic 'oriental' horror story, and *A Cavalry Tale (Reitergeschichte*, 1899), a historical sketch, probes the psychology of war behind external events in the manner and powerful syntax of Heinrich von Kleist. *Marshal de Bassompierre's Adventure (Das Erlebnis des Marschals von Bassompierre*, 1900) is based on a French anecdote about love and death that Hofmannsthal came across in Goethe. *Letter from Lord Chandos* (first published with the title *Ein Brief*, 1902) is part fiction, part philosophical epistle, while *Lucidor* (1910) is a piece of romantic comedy based on Molière and a preliminary sketch for the libretto of Strauss's *Arabella*. All these works are as richly suggestive and tightly choreographed as lyric poems, and display a thematic unity that endorses the view that there is considerable consistency of outlook behind Hofmannsthal's very varied opus. All of them might be described as secular variations on the Fall, tending to present characters as types, often with a classic fatal flaw. But if unlike Schnitzler's psychologically explicit fiction they are all, with the exception of *Lucidor*, removed from the immediate social world of *fin de siècle* Vienna, Hofmannsthal was at least as interested as Schnitzler in a typology of the mind. And like his near contemporary Joseph Conrad, he uses symbolism to explore the more elusive, unfathomable aspects of the human psyche. Commenting on Freud's *The Interpretation of Dreams* (1900) in one of his 'Vienna Letters' for the American journal *The Dial* in the 1920s, he wrote that it explored territory hitherto uncharted – except by poets.

Justice and *A Chance Glimpse of Happiness* are as different in mood and setting from each other as from Baudelaire's urban or Turgenev's allegorical prose poems, but both of them dramatise a fleeting encounter with and subsequent withdrawal from the ideal realm.[5] In *Justice*, an almost Blakean epiphany, the speaker is sitting in his garden amid falling blossoms – emblems of transience as in Japanese prints – when he is visited by a slender androgynous 'page of God', with golden hair and shoes made from the torn mantle of the Mother of God, who demands to know whether he is one of the just. Hofmannsthal apparently imagined him as like an angel by Mantegna, but he also seems a little dandified – even Beardsleyesque – as he stands toying with his hilt, and his imperious and uncompromising manner and adoring greyhound echo traits Hofmannsthal had found distasteful in George six months earlier. The angel's stern question, with its abstract Christian/Platonic pedigree and hint of election to a new post-Christian aestheticist élite, forces the speaker to examine both his own limitations and those of language itself in a way that anticipates *Letter from Lord Chandos*. The encounter is mutually unsatisfactory and the angel turns his back contemptuously and descends into the abyss. But a normative bridge between the ideal and the quotidian is suggested by the innocent wonderment of the gardener's child at the beauty of the angel's shoes. Hofmannsthal like the Romantics before him believed that only children and poets (and occasionally madmen) are capable of seeing the world whole.

In *A Chance Glimpse of Happiness*, a youthful travel experience such as Hofmannsthal might have had on his graduation trip to France is elevated into an encounter with ideal femininity – what Goethe called the 'eternal feminine', Novalis the mystical 'blue flower'. As he scents the receding Riviera coast and peoples the waves in imagination with antique deities, the first-person narrator suddenly spies another vessel sailing directly towards him. Through his glass – which brings the deck dramatically closer, suggesting an experience of ecstasy akin to that in

---

[5] For a detailed discussion of both these pieces, see Robert Vilain, *The Poetry of Hugo von Hofmannsthal and French Symbolism* (Oxford: Oxford University Press, 2000), pages 236–48.

Keats's odes 'To a Nightingale' and 'On a Grecian Urn' – he sees a lithe and beautiful young woman who seems strangely familiar. Yet he is unable to identify her with any specific woman of his acquaintance seen in the Prater or a theatre box. For she represents his anima or emanation, an ideal often intimated to him by the beauties of nature, the music of Schubert and certain passages of poetry which have seemed to hold the 'key to the golden gates of life'. (Again, the parallel with Keats's 'pleasure thermometer' of ascending ecstasy, from nature through music to love, is striking.[6]) He knows with a certainty that defies ordinary logic that with her he will be able to communicate in the winged language of art which transcends ordinary humdrum speech. But the encounter is all too fleeting, the ship named *Fortune* drifts away like Keats's nightingale, and the speaker is left desolate and empty. Imaginatively, this narrative has affinities with Hofmannsthal's early poem 'Experience' ('Erlebnis'), in which the speaker sees his own childhood double on the foreshore as he sails towards his death.

The next three works – *The Tale of the 672nd Night, A Cavalry Tale* and *Marshal de Bassompierre's Adventure* – despite their very different literary antecedents, were considered sufficiently akin by Hofmannsthal to publish in book form together with *Letter from Lord Chandos*, with the first of them providing the title of the volume, in 1905. If *Justice* and *Happiness* picture the ideal as remote and inaccessible, these tales are equally bleak and poignant in dramatising the fleetingness and futility of human desire and the suddenness, brutality and omnipotence of death in a post-Nietzschean world bereft of God. *The Tale of the 672nd Night* is particularly harrowing, and has as much in common

---

[6] See Earl R. Wasserman, *The Finer Tone: Keats' Major Poems* (Baltimore: Johns Hopkins University Press, 1953), pages 13f. and 178f., where Keats's use of this ascending scale of ecstasy in the imagery of 'Ode on a Grecian Urn' and 'Ode to a Nightingale' is discussed. On Hofmannsthal's reading of Keats, see Michael Hamburger, 'Hofmannsthal's Debt to the English-speaking World' in his *Hofmannsthal: Three Essays* (Princeton: Princeton University Press, 1972), pages 144–45.

with the internalised gothic horror tales of Tieck, Hoffmann and later Kafka as with the *Arabian Nights*. Schnitzler, in a letter to Hofmannsthal dated 26 November 1895, commented on its dream-like qualities – his own *Dream Story* (1926) begins with an oriental tale being read to a child – but observed that it lacked the warm glow of fairy-tales, and suggested a happy ending with the hero waking up.[7] And in a later essay, 'The Thousand and one Nights' ('Tausendundeine Nacht', 1907), Hofmannsthal paid tribute to the great classic as above all a sunny book, not a 'labyrinth ... full of the uncanny'. Thus by giving his own work the number of a non-existent tale in the oriental text, he hints perhaps that he is about to tell a darker and as yet untold story. Obliquely autobiographical and published late in the year of Oscar Wilde's trial – news of which had contributed to his depression while billeted in Göding – it is his most powerful indictment of aestheticism, which in an essay on Pater he called 'dangerous as opium'.

In the more richly tapestried prelapsarian first section, the merchant's son, a kindred soul to Huysmans' epicurean Des Esseintes and Wilde's narcissist Dorian Gray, having failed to find a bride, retreats to his artificial paradise in the hills. Here, under the watchful eyes of his four uncanny servants, he devotes his time to contemplating his beautiful possessions and – like many a Wagnerian or Preraphaelite – to idealising the remote heroic past, while unconsciously longing for death. In the second section, where the pace accelerates as if caught up in the slipstream of time, his sanctuary is disrupted by an anonymous letter accusing his valet of unspecified vile crimes. Leaving his garden to investigate, he is plunged into a nightmare world of *Doppelgänger*, Piranesiesque bridges – consistently a symbol of spiritual transition – and labyrinthine alleys which lead him inexorably to his violent and sordid nemesis, cursing his servants for having brought him to this pass. And from the outset the

---

[7] Hofmannsthal/Arthur Schnitzler, *Briefwechsel*, edited by Therese Nickl and Heinrich Schnitzler (Frankfurt: S. Fischer, 1964), pages 63–64.

suggestion is skilfully built up that they are not merely repre-
sentatives of a threatening servant class, but projections of inad-
equacies in his own emotional makeup, recreating that sense of
the instability of the ego and the fluid boundary between subject
and object that was so much in the air in late nineteenth-century
Vienna, under the influence of the ideas of the philosopher
Ernst Mach.[8] He vacillates for instance between empathising
with their lives more intensely than he experiences his own, and
regarding them – as if through glass – as silent alien creatures,
whose watchful eyes (a Hoffmannesque touch) make him more
conscious of his 'own secret inadequacy as a human being'. And
the way he catches fleeting glimpses of them – at a window or
in a mirror – contributes to the sense of this mental space as a
shifting hall of mirrors. The absence of direct dialogue between
them enhances the effect.

The three maid-servants, who collectively induce in him 'a
mortal fear of the ineluctability of life', have distinct affinities
with the three Norns who weave man's fate in Nordic myth and
are conventionally depicted as a crone (past), a mature woman
(present) and a maiden (future). This, if they are construed
as facets of the hero's psyche, would be consistent with
Hofmannsthal's comment in his 1905 essay 'Sebastian Melmoth',
that fate did not leap out at Oscar Wilde 'like a vicious dog':
his fate and his character were 'one and the same thing'. The
housekeeper, a mother surrogate with 'the chill of age' upon her,
seems linked to the merchant's son's nostalgia for the past and
secret longing to return to the womb. The beautiful languid older
maid is potentially a bride, yet she fills him with 'longing but
no desire'. At one point he glimpses her in a mirror apparently
descending from a higher realm (like the figures in *Justice* and
Happiness) but actually ascending from below, and bearing two
sinister serpentine Indian statuettes – all suggesting his very *fin*

---

[8] For a discussion of Mach's influence on Hofmannsthal and his Viennese
contemporaries, see Allan Janik and Stephen Toulmin, *Wittgenstein's Vienna*
(New York: Simon & Schuster, 1973), pages 81f., 116f. and 241.

de siècle ambivalence toward female sexuality. And in what has been described as a process of 'aestheticising' woman – exemplified in different ways from Dante through Novalis to Rossetti, Klimt and Morris – he exalts her in imagination into a young queen in battle and turns to seek her essence in a flower. The valet, with his suave solicitude and dusky 'mulberry-coloured' complexion appears to represent an emotional alternative to this Preraphaelite beauty, and the merchant's son, who has become as possessively attached to him as his father had been to his hard-earned wealth, takes the anonymous letter as a personal insult designed to 'force him to flee from himself and to repudiate all that he held dear'. The fierce moody suicidal younger maid, who corresponds to Grimm's account of the youngest, smallest and most malignant Norn, and whose sudden reappearance as her own double adds to the tale's uncanny Hoffmannesque effects, seems to embody all the regressive fear, fury and self-destructiveness within the protagonist. And her chewed lip and the wicked look she gives him anticipate those of the lethal horse and his own 'alien, evil expression' at the end of the tale.

With these essentially life-denying demons ruling his divided soul, the merchant's son finds himself wandering through a depressive mental wasteland toward the all-male world of the military barracks – a world dominated by the horse, as is vividly conveyed by the line of soldiers kneeling, as if in obeisance, washing their chargers' hooves. The merchant's son's ineptitude with horses, hinted at when he disavows all interest in an ornamental saddle in the pawnshop, is a measure of the distance between him as a representative decadent son of nineteenth-century affluence and the heroic age that he idealises. And with its traditional association with unbridled passion, nightmare and death, the horse he encounters at the end is an appropriate symbol both of the return of the repressed within him and of the brute realities of life he has tried to escape from into art. The malicious look it gives him, rendered more uncanny by the white patch running across its eyes like an allegorical Death's mask, triggers a fleeting but fatally distracting chain of early associations in his mind, first with a cornered thief, then with 'the sweet smell of warm peeled almonds', suggesting onanistic guilt. Thus the kick in the loins, clearly psychosexual, neatly brings together some of the story's wider associations – the essential sterility of the aesthete's way of life, the retributive violence of society witnessed in the Wilde case, and the bleakness of death in the post-Christian world. Hofmannsthal did not take much interest in expressionist writers or painters beyond Van Gogh, but the merchant's son's last hour must be among the most visually expressionistic death scenes ever penned.

A Cavalry Tale, while also drawing on Hofmannsthal's military experience, was directly inspired by a trip he made to historic sites in northern Italy in 1897, and is set during Austria's 1848 campaign against Italian insurgents led by Field Marshal Radetzky – the hero commemorated in the older Johann Strauss's famous *Radetzky March*. Despite their difference in genre, this story and *The Tale of the 672nd Night* almost form a diptych as regards characterisation, theme and narrative technique. In terms of class, occupation and temperament the central character, Sergeant Anton Lerch, is the merchant's son's complete antithesis – underprivileged, a seasoned horseman, and as one-sidedly instinctive, physical and violent as the aesthete is passive, contemplative and fearful. He too has a fatal flaw – an Adamic weakness which is the reverse of the merchant's son's gynophobia but as understandably the product of his circumstances. And in the course of an action which classically takes place within one day, it leads him as inexorably to an encounter with his double – by a bridge over a dry ditch – followed by sudden violent death. Again the pace is subtly varied, as if to suggest the changing speed of the horses, and the skirmish at sunrise and battle scene at sunset, each narrated with the brisk objectivity of a military report, symmetrically frame the two contrasting central sections – the triumphal entry into Milan and the slow surreal ride through a famine-stricken village. These both provide the grounding for Lerch's later insubordination, while as inner landscapes they reflect his elation after the morning's action and his dejection over unsatisfied desire. They also mirror the class structure against which he is subconsciously rebelling – the affluence he envies and the poverty he fears. Again, verbal communication between the characters is minimal.

Throughout the Milan episode there is an undercurrent of sex and violence which others too were to evoke as a concomitant of military life – notably Schnitzler in *Lieutenant Gustl* (1900) and Musil in *The Confusions of the schoolboy Törless* (1906). In the magniloquent opening panorama, the submerged image is of a beautiful defenceless city being ravished by the Austrian cavalry, their naked swords erect as pretty women open windows or are glimpsed enticingly through church doors. Lerch's chance encounter with the fair Vuic is similarly suggestive, invoking a wide range of intertextual echoes – of *The Romance of the Rose*, medieval knights waylaid by temptresses, or the iconography of Mars subdued by Venus. Catching sight of her at a window, he turns aside from the parade and strict military discipline, enters her courtyard, dismounts to ease his steed of an irritating stone, and is greeted by her in dishabille. Her clean-shaven older paramour, who plays Vulcan to their Mars and Venus and is glimpsed retreating in the peer-glass of her opulent apartment, is at once an obstacle, an object of envy and a projection of himself in the affluent retirement he aspires to.[9] He departs, vowing to billet with her in a week and savouring thoughts of 'ease and gratifying dominion' – with the hilt of his sabre poking out of his dressing-gown – and schemes for humiliating his rival. The entire encounter is a fleeting moment in the onward surge of events.

---

[9] Two paintings of Venus, Mars and Vulcan are suggestive here. In one, attributed to Giovanni da Udine in the Castel Sant' Angel in Rome, Venus by her bedside with her mirror is centrally located, with her back to a bearded Vulcan lying in wait in an inner room, and facing a more youthful Mars approaching from outside. In Jacopo Tintoretto's painting in the Munich Alte Pinakothek, Vulcan is seen unveiling Venus, while Mars hides under the bed and Cupid lies asleep, Vulcan's image also being reflected in a mirror. See Jan L. De Jong, 'Ovidian Fantasies: Pictorial variations in the story of Mars, Venus and Vulcan', in *Die Rezeption der Metamorphosen des Ovid in der Neuzeit*, edited by Hermann Walter and Hans-Jürgen Horn (Berlin: Gebr. Mann, 1995), pages 161–72.

Where the Milan sequence presents the pomp of war and the euphoric fantasies of an inarticulate and aggressive warrant officer, the ravaged village into which – again against regulations – Lerch now turns in search of easy glory reveals the ugly consequences of the Austrians' campaign, and (like the barracks in the previous story) objectifies the utter dejection and disgust with military life that suddenly comes over him. The increasingly halting advance of his horse suggests that all his vital energies are draining from him. And if the earlier coital imagery is being modulated – in the misfiring pistol, the faceless woman indifferent to the hard-breathing horse, its shying at the rats locked in fierce embrace, the pressure from Lerch's thighs urging it on – it is in demonic mode as in a Bosch engraving. The street mongrels might be construed as a bleak image of the blind warring prolixity of life, always teetering on the edge of chaos.

Lerch's encounter with his double comes at the nadir of this entropic sequence, where time seems to stand still and every step exhausts him – nightmare effects later used no less brilliantly by Kafka in *A Country Doctor* (1919). Instinctively – and in line with folk superstition – the horse picks up the uncanny presence first and emits a death-like sigh, the source of which Lerch's disoriented conscious mind is unable to detect – an anticipatory fracture as it were between soul and body. Like Shakespeare's tragic heroes, particularly Macbeth, he is subliminally afflicted by what Freud would later term the death wish. And once across the bridge he joins a blood-bath of extraordinary violence, accentuated by the setting sun, which from the vantage-point of 1914 has an apocalyptic, indeed prophetic aura. Thus Lerch's sudden blind mutinous rage against his commanding officer, Baron Rofrano, when ordered to surrender his high-stepping captured thoroughbred – described to suggest a vain and spirited woman – has been carefully prepared for, and the swift dénouement has a classical inevitability about it. Rofrano has been construed as Hofmannsthal's ideal man of action coolly restoring military order, but there is also implied criticism in his languid aristocratic callousness – tinged perhaps with class revenge for Lerch's killing an Italian brother officer, albeit on the enemy side.

Marshal de Bassompierre's Adventure is perhaps Hofmannsthal's most assured and satisfying story formally – he always found endings difficult – and it exemplifies his willingness to rework a plot from an earlier writer if he thought he could bring out its deeper resonances or contemporary relevance. It is a tale of adulterous passion set in the seventeenth century in time of plague, the bare bones of which are taken from Goethe's *Entertainments of German Refugees* (*Unterhaltungen deutscher Ausgewanderten*, 1795), he in turn having translated it from the memoirs (1665) of Marshal François de Bassompierre, a highly placed diplomat under Louis XIII. But Hofmannsthal expands the lovers' two assignations and enriches the parallels between them so that as contrasting moments of intense desire and mortal terror they encompass the emotional poles of human existence. And he ingeniously fills out the interval between them by affording the hero Bassompierre a glimpse of his mistress's husband as a fine-looking and far from pitiable man, thus enhancing the enigma of the woman's motives.[10] As a story about a casual sexual encounter *Bassompierre* is also Hofmannsthal's most Schnitzlerean story, and he may well have seen in the plague setting of his sources a convenient metaphor for the taboo subject of syphilis – much as Bram Stoker is thought to have used the vampire legend in his novel *Dracula* (1897).

As in *A Chance Glimpse of Happiness*, and as in both his models, Hofmannsthal presents the story from the first person point of view of Bassompierre himself, and this has the effect of making the anonymous woman the more tantalising for being – like the *fin de siècle* ladies Musil ridicules in the passage quoted earlier – shrouded in mystery. Certainly her forwardness at her shop under the sign of the two angels (Love and Death perhaps) near the Petit Pont leading into the heart of Paris – a Rubicon for

---

[10] See Hofmannsthal, *Four Stories,* edited by Margaret Jacobs (Oxford: Oxford University Press, 1968), pages 34–39.

them both – indicates that if she is still chaste she is by no means shy. And in portraying their fleeting relationship Hofmannsthal displays a sympathetic understanding of the differences between male and female responses to erotic passion, as well as of the class dimension, without however wholly disguising his ambivalence toward the new liberated woman.

Bassompierre, who is presented with increasingly apparent irony, initially takes a seigneurial attitude to the affair, treating it as an adventure with a temptress of the lower orders and taking rational precautions against the plague. During their preliminary lovemaking he even groggily confuses her with some other woman. For her, if her protestations and disdain for the procuress are taken at face value, this passion is something all-consuming and ennobling – indeed she appears to romanticise *eros* as fervently as the merchant's son romanticises *thanatos*. And in the climactic firelight scene, where the soaring flames evoke their passion and gestures take the place of words, she becomes a towering presence – a *femme fatale* who like Eve in Milton and Christian iconography takes the initiative – proffering the apple and fearlessly handling the 'stout log' that fuels the blaze.[11] They awake, in the *aubade* tradition, to a 'pale abhorrent dawn' in which the surreal wintry landscape both mirrors their post-coital sadness and suggests a chaotic post-lapsarian – indeed post-Christian – world where 'bogies roam'. Beautifully though this whole high Romantic sequence is done, it also contains a touch of hyperbole that suggests Hofmannsthal might be tilting at the cult of what he termed Wagnerian 'erotic screaming'.[12] And the woman's signs of shame and fear, her indignation over the proposed second meeting at the brothel, her mood swings and her ironic oath of fidelity all show her to be still as much a daughter of Eve as of Isolde.

---

[11] See Nina Berman, 'Hofmannsthal's Political Vision', in Kovach, pages 214–16.
[12] Quoted in Hofmannsthal, *Plays & Libretti*, page xxx.

In the second part of the story the mystery thickens and the tension steadily increases. Despite himself, Bassompierre now becomes obsessed, indeed classically blinded by passion for this extraordinary woman. And he is too overwhelmed by jealousy of her husband to decipher the latter's gesture as he examines his nails for signs of plague, or to link his resemblance to a noble prisoner once in his charge to the possibility that the woman might have infected him out of revenge.[13] The parallelism between the first and second assignations is deftly managed, as he crosses a second fateful bridge, like Sergeant Lerch 'seething with impatience' for the erotic delights he imagines awaiting him, and in a classic peripetia and anagnorisis, finds his ardour turning to terror at the sight of what has aptly been called a 'macabre travesty' of their night of passion, with the shadows from the straw fire rising and falling in mockery of carnal love and the whole Wagnerian notion of a *Liebestod*. To construe the plague as a metaphor for syphilis is to make the tale more moralistic, but it also gives the anonymity and mystery surrounding the woman and her husband a thematic relevance beyond its narratological effectiveness. One of the themes of Schnitzler's play *Round Dance* (1897) too is precisely the impersonality of sex. (However, unlike the promiscuous Schnitzler keeping count of his affairs and orgasms in his diary, Hofmannsthal, who as a youth confided his sexual anxieties to the older writer, appears to have led a chaste and happy married life.[14])

Letter from Lord Chandos is an experiment of a different kind, not unlike a Browning monologue in prose, in which Hofmannsthal projects a modern poet's existential-cum-linguistic crisis back into the Elizabethan age, historically another threshold era paralleling his own when traditional beliefs and forms were failing to account for new realities. But despite the absence of plot and the elevated rhetoric, this philosophical

---

[13] Berman, page 210.

[14] Discussed in Peter Gay, *Schnitzler's Century: The Making of Middle-class Culture 1815–1914* (New York: Norton, 2002), pages 63f.

epistle from a fictive Lord Chandos to the historical Francis Bacon is thematically linked to the other stories in that it again involves a central character's loss of innocence or fall from grace.[15] Bacon's appropriateness as Chandos's mentor is two-edged. On the one hand he is the Renaissance all-rounder that Chandos – and to a degree Hofmannsthal himself – aspires to be, having contributed to traditional humanist discourse with moral essays, *Apophthegms New and Old* (1625), an allegorical treatise *The Wisdom of the Ancients* (1609), and notes for a history of Henry VIII, all touching on Chandos's own creative ambitions. On the other hand, in the *Novum Organum* (1620) especially, he is the great iconoclast, advocating the demolition of the 'idols' of received wisdom through empirical investigation – the method that the Romantics proclaimed a blight on the imagination, that in Keats's words can 'unweave a rainbow' and 'clip an Angel's wings', that in Blake's view created the 'mind-forg'd manacles' of industrial civilisation, and that applied to language reduces Chandos to the brink of despair. In this sense, Chandos might be envisaged as addressing his own mirror image or demonic double – what Blake termed the doubting rationalist 'Spectre' within all of us.

Chandos's perspective as he writes is already a lapsarian one. But in reminding Bacon of Hippocrates' aphorism that 'he who is seriously ill yet feels no pain is sick in spirit' – no less applicable to *fin de siècle* Vienna – he also hints that his delving into his own 'unfathomable mind' in search of self-knowledge is cathartic. In the first part, an elegy for the demise of an integral world picture, Chandos describes how the 'mysteries of faith' have become as elusive as 'receding rainbows' and compares the self-referential wisdom of the Ancients to being 'locked in a garden amongst eyeless statues'. He complains that, under empirical scrutiny, he has found the meaning of key philosophical

---

[15] H. Stefan Schultz, 'Hofmannsthal and Bacon: the Sources of the Chandos Letter', *Comparative Literature*, 13 (1961), pages 1–15 concludes that Hofmannsthal's poet is not based on any specific historical figure.

words such as soul, body, truth or virtue disintegrating in his mouth like 'mouldy mushrooms'. And he finds that rhetoric, from Hofmannsthal's perspective the basis of the entire poetic tradition from Antiquity through the *Pléiade* poets to Victor Hugo, fails to 'penetrate to the heart of things'. The corrosive effect of this radical scepticism has been to deprive Chandos of the capacity to 'think or speak coherently about anything at all', reducing him to silence. As Hofmannsthal has Balzac prophesy in an essay 'On Characters in the Novel and in Drama' ('Über Charactere im Roman und im Drama', also written in 1902), modern poets' dissatisfaction with existing words as a vehicle for expressing their feelings would shortly reach a point of crisis. A contemporary linguistic philosopher, Fritz Mauthner, was concurrently working on a theoretical treatise that would endorse Hofmannsthal's insight and later provide the point of departure for Wittgenstein's *Tractatus Logico-Philosophicus*, arguing that all language is inherently metaphorical and all logical thinking psychologically biased and subjective.[16]

The visionary episodes Chandos describes in the longer second part of the *Letter* are in reaction to this philosophical and cultural impasse. In a slightly later essay, 'The Poet and this Time' ('Der Dichter und diese Zeit', 1906), Hofmannsthal observes that, however remarkable the achievements of science, only the poets can satisfy man's longing for a universe animated and unified by feeling. Chandos's account of his epiphanic experiences of humble things like wheelbarrows or basking dogs is an attempt to suggest in words the fact that sensory objects have an intense individuality and presence – what Hopkins termed their *haecitas* – which is not directly communicable in language. (Hofmannsthal's recognition of this is intimately connected to his increasing involvement with the theatre, which

---

[16] See Janik and Toulmin, pages 120–32. In correspondence with Mauthner after the publication of *Chandos*, Hofmannsthal denied any direct indebtedness to the linguistic scepticism of *Contributions to a Critique of Language* (1901–02), claiming to have reached his own views independently early in life.

with its many metalanguages could approach Wagner's ideal of the *Gesamtkunstwerk*, the total work of art, more closely than other literary forms.) His empathy with the abject rats he has ordered poisoned represents a triumph of the humanising imagination, while his shy reverence before the 'residual aura' of a nut tree and preference for a lowly shepherd's fire over the sublimity of the starry heavens are a plea for renewed awareness of the miraculousness of daily life – despite the absence of the cherubim he can't believe in. And when he identifies with Crassus and his absurd devotion to an eel, the episode lodges in his soul as a paradigm of the power and absurdity of love. Whereas the whirlpool created by the indeterminacy of words leads outward 'into the abyss', the whirlpool of love brings the cosmos back into the human heart. As Hofmannsthal wrote in his posthumously published notes *Ad me ipsum*, Chandos is a mystic without a theology. Chandos's farewell to literature in so far as he is his creator's spokesman is of course rhetorical, and his use of imagistic language points the way to its renewal. Hofmannsthal continued to write and to be infinitely fascinated by language – by the different connotations of the word 'genius' in English and in German, by the innumerable sociolects (diplomatic, military, aristocratic, metropolitan, suburban) current in Vienna in his time, by the folk dialect in the plays of Raimund and Nestroy, by the way a good translation can allow the naked beauty of the original to shine through like a dancer's figure through her veils. Indeed, in his last reflections on the community that the Habsburg Empire might have been, he reaffirms an almost mystical faith in language as a culturally healing, unifying force. And he recommends that the poet/prophet seeking to rebuild the spiritual New Jerusalem cast his linguistic net extremely widely – to the pre-Socratics, Orpheus and Lao Tse.

With *Lucidor* Hofmannsthal exchanges his prophetic for his comic mask, producing a delightful social comedy, indebted to *Twelfth Night* and Molière's *Le Dépit amoureux* for some of its plot machinations and gender reversals, and told with an elegance and irony which make it the most French in feel of all

these stories, despite the 1870s Vienna setting and the paucity of
dialogue. The situation is essentially the same as in the libretto
for Strauss's opera *Arabella*. The quixotic mother of two daughters decides to optimise her favourite Arabella's marital chances
and cut down on expenses by dressing up the younger daughter
Lucille as Lucidor, a boy. Complications set in however when
Lucille/Lucidor starts to write love letters to Arabella's suitor
Vladimir under her haughty sister's name. But whereas in the
opera the focus is on Arabella, and Strauss had Hofmannsthal
flesh out the social milieu with balls and duels that had musical
potential, *Lucidor* as the title implies is centrally about Lucille/
Lucidor's gradual self-discovery, and more broadly about the
importance of sexuality in bringing about personality integra-
tion and marital fulfilment for both sexes.

In some respects the story's love configurations are analogous
to those in Goethe's *Elective Affinities (Die Wahlverwandtschaften*,
1809), a novel which Hofmannsthal refers to with admiration
in his essays more than once. But again as in *The Tale of the
672nd Night*, the boundaries between individuals are not clear-
cut, an effect facilitated by the omniscient narrative perspective. Vladimir, like the traditional Hercules between Virtue and
Pleasure, vacillates between the scornful 'daytime' Arabella
and the yielding 'night time' Arabella, Lucille/Lucidor, each
mirroring the 'secret split' between the rational and sensual selves
within himself.[17] At the same time they are not only two facets of
womanhood but two types of woman that complement and mirror
one another, and here Hofmannsthal was much influenced by
Stendhal's portrayal of the two great loves in Julien Sorel's life in
Le Rouge et le Noir (1830). Lucille/Lucidor undoubtedly steals
our hearts as she emerges from tomboy adolescence into fully
sexual womanhood, her fall from conventional morality a truly
felix culpa, but Arabella too is humanised when she reveals an
elective affinity for Vladimir's rival, Imfanger. Vladimir's closing
tribute to the 'unconditionally devoted soul' who has granted

---

[17] See Ellen Ritter, 'Hofmannsthal's Narrative Prose', in Kovach, pages 69–70.

him the 'secret desires of his nature' could be construed as a restatement of old chivalric attitudes, or of the Schopenhaurian view of woman as essentially irrational – given new currency at the turn of the century by Johann Jakob Bachofen's matriarchal studies of woman as a chthonic force.[18] But the corollary to splitting woman into these day- and night-time facets is that ideally they should be united – that 'the same woman who was capable of giving herself so unreservedly should also know how to assert herself…'. At all events, *Lucidor* is Hofmannsthal's most sunny and optimistic story, one in which the cloud of sexual repression, sublimation and violence hanging over the characters in the other tales is lifted – a poignantly felicitous creative moment, as it were, before his own and the world's troubles descend in earnest.

---

[18] Gertrud Lehnert, *Wenn Frauen Männerkleider Tragen: Geschlecht und Maskerade in Literatur und Geschichte* (Munich: Deutscher Taschenbuch, 1997), page 98 considers Lucille's disguise a 'classic male fantasy' in that as Lucidor she becomes invisible as an object of desire to other men.

Translator's Note

CONSIDERING Hofmannsthal's linguistic gifts and international outlook, and the high quality of much of his work, it is ironic that only a fraction of it is currently available in English, despite the excellent pioneering translations by Michael Hamburger, Mary Hottinger, and Tania and James Stern in the 1950s and '60s. The seven stories and sketches translated in this book are among Hofmannsthal's most intriguing completed short works of fiction, as the volume of critical commentary devoted to them amply testifies. They have not been grouped together before in English, though some have made individual appearances, recent examples being Michael Hofmann's translation *The Lord Chandos Letter* (Penguin, 1995) and Mike Mitchell's translation of *Reitergeschichte* in his *Daedalus Book of Austrian Phantasy* (2003) under the title *Sergeant Anton Lerch*. My aim has been to reproduce Hofmannsthal's style and sentence structure while also trying to render the poetic density of these subtly nuanced texts.

The range of Hofmannsthal's literary activities prevented him from developing a formula for his fiction as did say Maupassant or Schnitzler, and the translator of his stories becomes very aware of his chameleon qualities as a self-consciously experimental stylist. The parabolic simplicity of *Justice*, the massive Kleistian syntax of *A Cavalry Tale*, the Elizabethan stateliness of *Letter from Lord Chandos*, the irony and wit of *Lucidor* all require their own adjustments of vocabulary, pace and cadence. Even within individual stories there can be considerable stylistic variation. The first part of *The Tale of the 672nd Night*, for instance, is deliberately static, ornate and lyrical, but in the eerie second part the pace becomes steadily more frenetic, and the finale is both surreal and starkly naturalistic. *A Cavalry Tale* opens with clipped military briskness, but at once proceeds to a panoramic description of the cavalrymen's triumphal ride through Milan. To make this magnificent long sentence more readable by dividing it into three, or by bringing the culminating main verb to the beginning, would be to destroy the sense of sights unfolding moment by moment as the squadron moves inexorably on; and there are similar arguments to be made against cutting the galloping syntax of the final battle scene down to size.

In *Letter from Lord Chandos,* Hofmannsthal's interlocking syntax translates quite readily into a simulacrum of the courtly Elizabethan English it is intended to invoke. But one is confronted with the very problem of linguistic indeterminacy the piece discusses, reminding one at every turn that, especially at a lexical level, translation involves interpretation and incurs the risk of imposing meanings not intended by the writer. The risk of over-interpretation is also high in *Marshal de Bassompierre's Adventure* because the tale is so suggestive, and sometimes there is a temptation to choose words that might exaggerate the extent to which the heroine is not merely a *femme fatale* but an uncanny figure.

Hofmannsthal's gift for concise expression, which carries over from his lyric poetry, often calls for amplification in English and sometimes creates insuperable conundrums. The title *Das Glück am Weg*, with its play on the double meaning of *Glück* as 'happiness' and 'luck', wonderfully sums up the essence of the story. This can be achieved only periphrastically in English, and *A Chance Glimpse of Happiness* is cumbersome, even when 'along the way' is left out as understood. Conversely, Hofmannsthal's interest in the metalanguages of dance and mime and the eloquence of the human face is often reflected in very specific descriptions of gestures, glances and expressions, which left unpruned in English are apt to sound hilarious.

Hofmannsthal's vocabulary in these stories is extensive but not technical, except for some military terminology in *A Cavalry Tale*. In *Lucidor* he uses a number of French and other foreign derivatives such as *vague, posieren* and *desavouieren* to enhance the sense of cosmopolitan sophistication, an effect largely lost in English translation. Foreign imports have always been more common in Austrian than in standard German, though interestingly Hofmannsthal was obliged to radically reduce the number of foreign words in his story before publication.

The text used for these translations, by kind permission of the publishers, was that of *Das Erzählerische Werk* (Frankfurt am Main: S. Fischer Verlag, 1969), taken from *Gesammelte Werke in Einzelausgaben,* edited by Herbert Steiner et al. (1945ff.). The biographical information given in the Introduction has been gleaned from many sources, but particularly from Werner Volke, *Hugo von Hofmannsthal in Selbstzeugnissen und Bilddokumenten* (Reinbek bei Hamburg: Rowohlt Verlag, 1967); references have been confined to the most directly salient sources as a matter of editorial policy. Some of the end-notes to the tales draw on *Sämtliche Werke: Kritische Ausgabe,* edited by Rudolf Hirsch (Frankfurt am Main: S. Fischer Verlag, 1975f.).

I should, finally, like to thank my publisher Antony Wood, Professor Ritchie Robertson, and my wife Poh Pheng for their astute criticism and suggestions.

J. M. Q. Davies
Bowness-on-Windermere, June 2006

Selected Tales

Justice

I WAS SITTING in the garden. Before me the gravel path led up through two pale green meadows to the brow of the hill, where the dark green, painted lattice fence was sharply etched against the bright spring sky. Where the path ended there was a little gate in the fence. In the thin pellucid air bees hovered here and there among the profusion of rosy pink peach blossoms. All at once the lattice gate creaked and a dog, a tall long-legged dainty greyhound, leaped into the garden. Behind it, closing the little gate behind him, came an angel, a slim blond youthful angel, one of the slender Pages of God. He was wearing pointed shoes, and had a long rapier at his side and a dagger in his belt. His breast and shoulders were clad in fine steel-blue armour with the sunlight playing on it, and white petals fell on his long thick gold-blond hair. He came on down the gravel path, a slight finely-made figure in a tightly-fitting emerald green jacket, the sleeves flounced above the elbow, tight from there to his elegant wrists. He walked slowly, gracefully, his left hand toying with the hilt of his dagger; the dog pranced about in the grass beside its master, looking up at him devotedly from time to time. By now he was no further away than a five-year-old can throw a ball.

'Will he speak to me if he comes over?'

The gardener's young child, playing in the meadow with the fallen blossom, now toddled over to the angel and looked at his feet: 'You have pretty shoes, very pretty!' 'Indeed,' said the angel, 'they are made from the mantle of the Mother of God.'

Then I saw that his shoes were of gold fabric woven with

a pattern of red flowers or fruit. 'Once the holy apostle Peter ran after the Mother of God,' the angel explained to the child, 'because he had something to tell her, but she didn't hear him calling and didn't stop. So then he hurried after her and in his haste stepped on her trailing mantle, tearing a piece off. Then the mantle was put aside and cut up into shoes for us.' 'The shoes are very pretty!' said the child again. Then the angel walked on down the gravel path which would lead him past my bench. An inexpressible elation came over me at the thought that he was going to speak to me as well. For there was an aura to the simple words that rose to his lips, as though he were thinking about something completely different, thinking secretly and with suppressed jubilation of the delights of paradise. Now he was standing before me. I rose and took off my hat to greet him. When I looked up I was startled by the expression on his face. His features were wonderfully refined and handsome, but the look in his deep blue eyes was grim, almost menacing, and his golden hair did not seem natural, but gave out an uncanny metallic gleam. The dog stood beside him, one forepaw raised daintily, and looked at me too with its attentive eyes.

'Are you a just man?' asked the angel severely. His tone was arrogant, almost contemptuous. I tried to smile: 'I am not a bad man. I am fond of lots of people. There are so many beautiful things.' 'Are you a just man?' asked the angel again. It was as though he had not heard what I had said; there was an edge of imperious impatience to his words, as when one repeats an order to a servant who has not understood at once. With his right hand he drew his dagger just a little from its sheath. I became uneasy; I tried to understand him, but without success; my mind went numb, unable to grasp the vital meaning of his words; a blank wall arose before my inner eye; in torment I tried in vain to think of something. 'I have grasped so little about life,' I blurted out at last, 'but sometimes I am inspired by ardent love and then nothing is alien to me. And then I certainly am just: for then I feel as if I could understand everything – how the earth puts forth rustling trees and how the stars hang suspended and revolve in space, and the quintessential nature of all things, and all the emotions of humanity . . .'

I faltered at his contemptuous look, and such a devastating consciousness of my inadequacy came over me that I could feel myself blushing with shame. His look said clearly: 'What an odious hollow chatterer!' There was not a trace of sympathy or reciprocity in it. A disdainful smile distorted his thin lips. He turned to go. 'Justice is everything,' he said. 'Justice is first and justice is last. Whoever does not understand this will die.' Whereupon he turned his back on me and with a spring in his step took the path down the hill, vanished behind the honey-suckle, reappeared, then finally descended the stone steps, disappearing little by little, first his slender legs below the knee, then his hips, and finally his shoulders clad in dark armour, his golden hair and emerald green cap. Behind him ran the dog, its dainty contours sharply outlined as it paused on the topmost step before leaping with one bound into the invisible.

A Chance Glimpse of Happiness

I WAS SITTING on some thick rope wound between two bollards in a deserted corner of the quarter-deck and looking back. Astern, the Riviera had become submerged in milky opaline fragrance – the yellowish slopes with ragged shadows of dark palms, the white flat houses nestling in huge clumps of rambler roses. Now that it had disappeared, I saw all this sharply and distinctly, and thought I could smell the delicate fragrance, the double fragrance of the sweet roses and the salty, sandy beaches. Yet the wind was blowing in towards the land, sweeping darkly across the smooth, wine-coloured expanse towards the land. So my thinking I could smell that fragrance can only have been an illusion. Then, where the broad band of the sun lay golden on the water, three dolphins leapt out, scattering showers of gold, chased one another gravely in their headlong rush, and suddenly dived again beneath the waves. The empty spot again became smooth and gleaming. Thus cart-wheeling clowns and jugglers dance before a festive procession, thus drunken, goat-hoofed fauns once pranced before Bacchus and his chariot ...

Now the water should have begun to seethe and, like the burrowing mole as it throws up soft ripples of soil and raises its head above the earth, the dripping manes and rosy nostrils of dappled horses should have appeared, followed by the white hands, arms and shoulders of nereids with their flowing hair, and the scalloped droning conches of Tritons. And there, holding the red silken reins festooned with dripping seaweed and green algae, Neptune himself should have been standing in his chariot of shell, not the tedious black-bearded porcelain god they make of him in Meissen, but uncanny and enticing like the sea itself, with infinite grace, feminine features and lips red as a poisonous red flower . . .

The soft wind swept darkly across the gleaming empty sea. On the horizon, not quite where the craggy coast of Corsica would appear as a blue-black streak when night came, a tiny black speck appeared.

An hour later the vessel had approached quite close to ours. It was a yacht that was evidently making for Toulon. We would almost touch as we passed. With good eyesight the mast and yardarms could already clearly be made out, and even the gilt mounting where the name of the boat was painted. I left my seat, took my English novel back to the reading-room and fetched my binoculars. They were an excellent pair and brought a clear round portion of the unknown yacht up close, almost eerily close. It was like looking through the window of a ground-floor room where people one has never seen before and will probably never meet are moving; yet for a moment one eavesdrops on them in their narrow stuffy room and feels incredibly close to them.

The disc in my binoculars was framed by dark rigging, brass-mounted planks, and beyond, the deep blue sky. In the middle there was a sort of camp-bed on which a fair-haired young lady was lying with her eyes closed. I could see everything distinctly: the dark cushion the heels of her light little shoes were digging into, the broad moss-green belt with a couple of half-opened roses tucked into it, pink roses, La France roses . . .

Was she asleep?

Sleeping people have a distinctive naiveté, an innocent and dreamlike charm. They never look unnatural or banal.

She was not asleep. She opened her eyes and bent to retrieve a fallen book. Her gaze passed over me and I became embarrassed to be staring at her at such close quarters; I lowered the binoculars, and only then did it occur to me that of course she was a long way off, to the naked eye no more than a pale dot against brown planks, and could not possibly have noticed me. So I again trained the binoculars on her, and now she was gazing straight ahead in a kind of reverie. At that moment I was sure of two things: that she was very beautiful and that I knew her. But how? It all came over me – vague, sweet, dear and from the past. I attempted to recall more clearly: a certain little garden where I had played as a child, with white gravel paths and begonia beds . . . but no, that wasn't it . . . then she too would of course have been a little child . . . a theatre, a box with an old woman and two girlish heads like bright bending flowers behind a fence . . . a carriage in the Prater on a spring morning . . . or had it been on horseback? . . . And the strong smell of dew-drenched bark, the scent of chestnut blossoms, and a certain ringing laugh . . . but that was someone else's . . . a certain boudoir with a little fireplace and a high Louis the Fifteenth fire-screen . . . all this resurfaced and instantly dissolved, and in each of these pictures appeared the shadowy image of the figure out there, whom I knew and did not know, that radiant slender figure with the tired loveliness of her small flower-like head and those dark, fascinating, mystic eyes . . . But she never coalesced in any of the pictures, ever and again dissolving, and my futile quest became intolerable. So I didn't know her after all. The thought caused me an inexplicable feeling of disappointment and inner emptiness; it was as though I had missed the best portion of my life. Then it dawned on me: yes, indeed I knew her, not as one normally knows people, but all the same, I had thought of her a hundred times, many hundreds, and for years and years.

Certain kinds of music had spoken to me of her very distinctly, particularly Schumann; certain evenings on violet-strewn green meadows beside a rushing stream beneath a rosy, humid evening sky; certain flowers, anemones with tired little heads . . . certain rare passages of poetry which make one look up with one's chin resting in one's hand, and suddenly the golden gates of life appear to open before one's inner eye . . . All these things had spoken to me of her, the phantom of her being had dwelt in all of them as the phantom of heaven dwells in the devout prayers of young children. And in all my secret longings she had been my secret goal: something in her presence gave everything meaning, something ineffably soothing, satisfying, crowning. One does not *understand* such things: suddenly one *knows* them.

Indeed, I knew far more than this; I knew I would converse with her in a very special language, special in tone and special in style: my speech would be more light-hearted, winged and free, it would set out as if sleepwalking along a narrow plank; it would also be more incisive and ceremonious, and certain harmonies would accompany it and give it added strength.

I did not think all these things through clearly, I saw them in a vague, fleeting picture language.

By this time the unknown vessel had come very close; it would scarcely be able to come much closer.

I knew even more about her: I knew her movements, the way she held her head, how she would smile when I said certain things to her. If she were sitting on the terrace of a little sea-side villa in Antibes (for no particular reason I thought especially of Antibes), and I were to come out of the garden and stand three steps below her (and I felt I knew for certain this would occur a hundred times, almost indeed that it had occurred already ...), then raising her shoulders in an indefinably charming little gesture, as if feeling cold, she would gaze down at me through her mystic eyes with a serious and gently mocking air ...

There is such a wealth of meaning in gestures: they are the complex, finely tuned language of the body for the soul's complex, refined quest for pleasure, which is both a kind of need for love and a kind of artistic urge; coquetry is a very rough and ready word for it. To me that little shrug of hers expressed an infinity of things: a particular way of being serious, contented and happy about beauty; a particular free, gracious, wholesome way of living; but above all, it seemed to express my happiness, to guarantee my own deep, calm, unquestionable happiness. All these notions of mine were replete with quiet certainty and grace, and quite without sentimentality. Meanwhile I continued to gaze across at her. She had got up and was looking directly at us. And then I had the impression that, with a quiet and scarcely perceptible smile, she shook her head. Immediately I noticed

with a sort of dull ache that the two boats were gently beginning to draw apart again. I did not register this as something
self-evident, nor as a painful surprise, it was simply as if my
very life, my entire being and memory were slipping away as the
yacht glided slowly, silently off, tearing the deep roots out of my
reeling soul, leaving nothing behind save infinite, idiotic emptiness. With a shiver, I thought I felt a gust of wind sweep through
this emptiness. Impassively, unthinkingly alert, I looked on as
an empty strip of pure, gleaming enamel-blue water opened
up between her and me and grew steadily wider. Anxiously
and helplessly I watched her slender supple figure as step by
step she slowly descended a little stairway, first her green belt
disappearing down the hatchway, then her delicate shoulders,
then her deep golden hair. Then nothing more of her remained,
nothing. To me it was as though she had been placed in a narrow
little trench, covered with a heavy stone and then grassed over.
As though she had been consigned to the dead and could no
longer mean anything at all to me. As I was staring in this way
at the receding vessel, which had altered course a little, something gleaming below deck-level was turned towards me. It was
the gilded group of putti, the golden guardian spirits wrought
on the ship's side and bearing a plate with the ship's name in
gleaming letters, *La Fortune* . . .

The Tale of the 672nd Night

I

A VERY HANDSOME young merchant's son, who had lost both
father and mother, shortly after turning twenty-five grew
weary of society and a life of entertaining. So he locked up
most of the rooms in his house and dismissed all his maids and
servants, except for four whose loyalty and general demeanour
pleased him. As his friends meant little to him, and no woman's
beauty had captivated him enough to make him consider it desir-
able or even tolerable to have her permanently by him, he grew
more and more accustomed to a life of virtual solitude, which
seemed best suited to his temperament. He was by no means a
recluse however, in fact he enjoyed strolling through the streets
and public parks observing people's faces. And he neglected
neither the care of his body and beautiful hands nor the decora-
tion of his home. Indeed, the beauty of his carpets, silks and
fabrics, his carved and panelled walls, his metal lamps and bowls,
his glass and his earthenware collection came to mean more to
him than he would ever have imagined. Gradually he came to
appreciate how his beloved objects contained all the shapes
and colours in the world. In intertwining ornaments he came
to recognise an enchanted image of the interconnected marvels
of the world. He discovered the forms of animals and the forms
of flowers, and the merging of flowers into animals; the shapes of
dolphins, lions and tulips, of pearls and acanthus; he discovered
the tension between the weight of columns and the resistance
of firm ground, the tendency of water always to rise and then
descend; he discovered the bliss of motion and the sublimity of

rest, dance and death; he discovered the colours of flowers and leaves, the colours of the furs of wild animals and the complexions of the different human races, the colours of precious stones, the colour of stormy and calm radiant seas; yes, he discovered the moon and the stars, the mystic sphere, the mystic rings, and consubstantial with these, the wings of seraphim. For a long time he was intoxicated by the immense, profound beauty that belonged to him, and he passed his days less emptily, more beautifully among these objects, which were no longer something dead and commonplace, but a great heritage, the divine work of all the generations of mankind.

And yet, he felt the futility as much as the loveliness of all these things; the thought of death never left him for long, often coming over him in the company of laughing noisy people, often at night, often during a meal.

But as he had no ailments, the thought was never terrifying; rather it had something festive and ceremonial about it, and came to him most forcefully when he was intoxicating himself with beautiful thoughts, or the beauty of his own youth and loneliness. For the merchant's son often took pride in his own image in the mirror, in the verse tributes of poets, in his wealth and his intelligence, and gloomy maxims did not weigh upon his soul. 'Where it is your destiny to die, your feet will carry you,' he would say, and imagine himself a king lost out hunting in the forest, advancing through strange trees toward some wondrous unknown fate. 'When the house is finished, Death will come,' he would say, and would see Death coming slowly over the bridge supported by winged lions to the palace, the finished house, overflowing with the wonderful bounty of life.

He imagined he would now be living completely alone, but his four servants circled him like dogs, and though he seldom spoke to them, he somehow felt they were incessantly thinking about how best to serve him. And so now and then he began to think about them too.

The housekeeper was an elderly woman; her deceased daughter had been wet-nurse to the merchant's son, and all her other children had died too. She was very quiet, and the chill of age emanated from her white face and her white hands. But he was fond of her because she had always been about the house, and because the memory of his own mother's voice and of his childhood, for which he had a nostalgic longing, was attached to her.

With his permission she had brought a distant relative to live with them, a girl who was scarcely fifteen years old and very withdrawn. She was hard on herself and difficult to understand. Once, prompted by some sudden dark impulse of her angry soul, she had thrown herself out of a window into the courtyard, but her child's body happened to land on a heap of earth, and she only broke her collarbone because a stone was hidden in it. When they had put her to bed, he sent his physician up to her, but in the evening he himself came to see how she was. Her eyes were shut, and for the first time he looked at her calmly for a while, and was astonished at the strange and prematurely knowing charm of her face. Only her lips seemed disagreeable, very thin and somehow uncanny. Suddenly she opened her eyes, gave him an icy wicked look, and angrily biting her lips to overcome the pain, turned towards the wall but in doing so rolled onto her injured side. Immediately her deathly pale face turned a greenish white and she became unconscious, falling back into her original position as if dead.

For a long time after she recovered, the merchant's son did not speak to her when he came upon her. He asked the housekeeper more than once whether the girl disliked living in his house, but she always replied in the negative. The only manservant he had decided to retain in his household he had come to know when dining once with the envoy whom the king of Persia maintained in the city. The man had served him at table and shown such discretion and civility, and at the same time been so reserved and modest, that the merchant's son found more pleasure in observing him than in listening to the conversation of the other guests. So he was all the more delighted when many months later this servant came up to him in the street and, without the slightest importunity, greeted him and offered him his services. The

merchant's son recognised him at once by his dusky mulberry-
coloured complexion and his well-bred manner. He immediately
took him into his service, discharging two young servants who
were still with him, and from then on would be served at meals
and such by this reserved and serious person alone. The man
was permitted to leave the house in the evening, but almost never
took advantage of this privilege. Indeed, he showed an unusual
devotion to his master, anticipating his wishes and silently
intuiting his dislikes and inclinations, so that the latter developed an even greater fondness for him.

But even though he would allow himself to be served only by
this man at meals, a maidservant would bring in the fruit and
pastries, a young girl, though two or three years older than the
child. This girl was the type that if seen by torchlight or from
a distance joining the dance would scarcely be considered beautiful, since then the refinement of her features would be lost;
whereas seeing her daily at close quarters, he was captivated
by the incomparable beauty of her eyelids and her lips, and the
languid joyless movements of her lovely body seemed to him the
enigmatic language of a closed and marvellous world.

When the summer heat became intense in the city, and the rows
of houses emitted a dull glare, and in the sultry oppressive night
under a full moon the wind blew white dust clouds through the
streets, the merchant's son would travel with his four servants to
a country chalet he owned in the mountains, situated in a narrow
valley surrounded by dark crags. There were many such houses
there, belonging to the rich. On either side waterfalls cascaded
down into the gorges, disseminating coolness. The moon was
almost always hidden behind the mountains, but great white
clouds rose behind the black cliffs, floated ceremoniously across
the luminous dark sky and vanished on the other side. Here
the merchant's son lived his customary life, in a house whose
wooden walls were always permeated with the cool fragrance of
the gardens and the many waterfalls. In the afternoons, until the
sun went down behind the mountains, he would sit in his garden
reading, usually a book in which the wars of some very great

king from the past were chronicled. Sometimes, in the middle of a description of how thousands of the enemy kings' cavalry turned their steeds in clamorous flight, or how their chariots were swept down a steep river bank, he would suddenly have to pause, for without looking up he sensed that the eyes of his four servants were fixed upon him. Without lifting his head he knew that they were silently watching him, each from a different room. How well he knew them. He could feel them living more intensely, more insistently than he could himself. He occasionally felt mildly emotional or surprised about himself, but concerning them he felt unaccountably oppressed. With the distinctness of a nightmare he sensed how the two older servants were advancing toward death, with every hour, with every stealthy inexorable alteration of those features and expressions he knew so well; and how the two young girls were advancing into their desolate and as it were airless lives. The burden of their lives, which they themselves were unaware of, oppressed him like the horror and deathly bitterness of a nightmare forgotten upon waking.

Sometimes he had to get up and walk about in order not to succumb to his terror. But as he gazed at the harsh gravel beneath his feet, and with all his might tried to concentrate on the fragrance of the gillyflowers mingling with the mild, over-sweet clouds of fragrance from the heliotropes that ascended from the cool fragrance of the grass and soil, he could feel their eyes on him and could think of nothing else. Without raising his head he sensed that the old woman was sitting at her window, her bloodless hands on the sun-drenched sill, her bloodless, mask-like face an even more gruesome setting for the helpless dark eyes that could not die. Without raising his head he sensed when his manservant withdrew from his window for some minutes and busied himself at a cupboard; without looking up he awaited the moment of his return with secret dread. As he let supple branches close behind him with both hands, and crept away into the most overgrown corner of the garden to concentrate all his thoughts on the beauty of the sky piercing through the dark network of tendrils and branches in bright little patches

of moist turquoise, what alone possessed his entire consciousness and blood was the knowledge that the eyes of the two girls
were directed at him – those of the older one languid, sorrowful
and vaguely demanding in a way that tortured him, those of the
younger one impatiently or else contemptuously watchful in a
way that tormented him still more. And yet as he went about
with his head bowed, or knelt in front of the gillyflowers to tie
them up with raffia, or ducked beneath the branches, he never
thought they were watching him directly; rather it was as though
they were watching his entire life, his deepest being, his secret
inadequacy as a human being.

A terrible feeling of oppression overcame him, a morbid fear
of the ineluctability of life. More terrible than their incessant
watching was the fact that they forced him to think about himself
in such a wearisome unfruitful way. And the garden was much
too small to get away from them. Yet when he was at all close to
them his fear vanished so completely that he almost forgot about
the past. Then he would succeed in taking no notice of them
or in calmly observing their movements, which were so familiar
that they made him feel a constant, almost physical sense of
empathy with their lives.

The younger girl he came across only now and then, on the
stairs or in the hall. The other three however were frequently in
the same room with him. Once he caught sight of the older girl
in a tilted mirror; she was going through an adjoining room on a
higher level, but in the mirror she seemed to come towards him
from below. She was walking slowly and with an effort, but very
upright: in each arm she was carrying a heavy bronze statue of a
gaunt Indian deity. She supported the ornate feet of these dusky
goddesses in her palms, so that they extended from her hips to
her temples, their dead weight resting against her delicate living
shoulders; while their dark heads with evil serpent's mouths and
three wild eyes in their foreheads, and sinister ornamentation in
their hard cold hair, moved alongside her breathing cheeks and
brushed her lovely temples in time with her slow steps. And yet
it did not seem to be the heavy goddesses that she was carrying

so ceremoniously, but rather the beauty of her own head with its heavy embellishment of dark living gold, two great coils on either side of her fair forehead, like a queen in battle. He was captivated by her great beauty, but at the same time he recognised quite clearly that it would mean nothing to him to hold her in his arms. He was altogether certain that the beauty of this maidservant filled him with longing but with no desire, so that he did not let his glance linger on her long, but left the room, indeed went out into the street and in strange disquiet walked in the narrow shade between the houses and gardens. Finally he went down to the river bank where the gardeners and florists lived, and for a long while sought – although he knew that he would seek in vain – for a flower with a form and fragrance, or a spice with an evanescent aroma, that would for one moment grant him quiet enjoyment of precisely the same sweet sensation that he had found so bewildering and unsettling in the beauty of his maidservant. And as he peered in vain among the gloomy greenhouses with longing in his eyes, and bent across the long flower beds over which dusk was already falling, involuntarily, indeed tormentingly and quite against his will, the lines of the poet kept running through his head: 'In the stems of gillyflowers as they swayed, in the fragrance of ripe corn you aroused my longing; but when I found you, you were not the one I had been seeking but the sisters of your soul.'

II

About this time he happened to receive a letter that disturbed him somewhat. The letter was unsigned. Obscurely the writer accused his manservant of having committed some revolting crime while still in the house of his former master, the Persian envoy. The unknown person seemed to bear a bitter grudge against the servant and made several threats, even adopting a discourteous, almost threatening tone towards the merchant's son himself. But there was no guessing what crime was being hinted at or what conceivable purpose this letter could serve

the writer, who neither named himself nor made any demands.
The merchant's son read the letter several times and admitted
to himself that he felt extremely apprehensive at the thought of
losing his servant in so disagreeable a way. The more he reflected,
the more agitated he became and the less he could tolerate the
idea of losing any one of these beings who through habit and
other mysterious forces had grown so utterly a part of him.

He paced up and down and his angry agitation made him so
hot that he threw off his coat and belt and trampled on them.
He felt as though someone had insulted and threatened his most
cherished inner possessions, and was trying to force him to flee
from himself and to repudiate all that he held dear. He was
consumed with self-pity and, as always at such moments, felt
like a child. Already he could see his four servants dragged from
his house and he felt as if the entire content of his life were being
silently ripped out of him, all his bitter-sweet memories, all his
half-unconscious expectations, everything he could not express,
to be cast away like a clump of seaweed. For the first time he
understood something that had always roused his anger as a boy,
the fearful love with which his father had clung to what he had
acquired, the riches of his vaulted warehouse, the beautiful,
unfeeling progeny of his quest and care, the mysterious offspring
of the deepest obscure desires of his life. And he understood why
the very great king from the past would have been bound to die
if he had been deprived of the lands he had traversed from coast
to coast and conquered, the lands he had dreamed of ruling but
which were so vast he neither had power over them nor received
tribute from them beyond the satisfaction that he had conquered
them and that nobody but he was their king.

He resolved to do everything necessary to lay this matter that
worried him so much to rest. Without saying a word about the
letter to the servant, he got himself ready and drove down to
the city alone. There he decided first of all to call at the house
where the Persian envoy lived, vaguely hoping to find some clue
there.

But when he arrived it was late in the afternoon and no one

was at home, neither the envoy nor any of the young people on his staff. Only the cook and an old assistant scribe were sitting in the doorway in the cool twilight. But they were so ugly and made such sullen replies that he turned his back on them impatiently and decided to come again at a better time next day.

As his own residence was locked up – he had left no servants behind in town – he had to think about finding lodging for the night like any stranger. Curiously, like a stranger, he walked through the familiar streets and finally came to the bank of a little river, which at that time of year had almost dried up. From there, lost in thought, he followed a wretched street inhabited by prostitutes. Without paying much attention to where he was going, he then turned to the right and found himself in an utterly deserted deathly quiet cul-de-sac, which ended in a steep flight of steps almost the height of a tower. He paused on the steps and looked back the way he had come. He could see into the yards of the little houses; here and there were red curtains in the windows and ugly dust-covered flowers; the broad dry river-bed had a deathly sadness about it. He continued climbing and at the top entered a district he could not remember ever having been in before. And yet the intersection of two sordid streets suddenly seemed familiar, as in a dream. Walking on he came to a jeweller's shop. It was a very dingy shop in keeping with that part of the city, and the window was filled with the kind of worthless trinkets that may be bought from pawnbrokers and receivers of stolen goods. The merchant's son, who was a connoisseur of precious stones, could scarcely find a passably attractive stone among them.

Suddenly, his glance fell on an old-fashioned piece of delicate gold jewellery ornamented with a beryl, which somehow reminded him of the old woman. He had probably seen a similar piece in her possession dating from her youth. The pale, almost melancholy stone also seemed in some strange way to suit her age and looks, and the old-fashioned setting had the same air of sadness. So he entered the low-ceilinged shop to buy the piece. The jeweller was very pleased to see such a well-dressed customer come in, and was keen to show him his more valuable gems which he did not display in the window. Out of courtesy to the old man he let himself be shown a good many things but had neither the desire to buy anything more nor would have had any use for such objects in his solitary life. Eventually he became both embarrassed and impatient, wanting to get away without hurting the old man's feelings. He decided to purchase one more small item and then leave at once. Looking absent-mindedly over the jeweller's shoulder, he considered a little silver hand-mirror, so tarnished as to be half-blind. Then from another mirror within him, the image of the maidservant flanked by the dark heads of the bronze goddesses advanced towards him; fleetingly he sensed that a great deal of her charm lay in the way the modest child-like grace of her shoulders and neck bore the beauty of her head, the head of a young queen. And fleetingly he thought how beautiful a delicate gold chain would look around that neck, wound round and round, child-like and yet reminiscent of chain-mail. And so he asked to see a few such chains. The old man opened a door and invited him into a second room, a low sitting-room where however a lot of jewellery was on display in glass cabinets and open cases. Here he soon found a little chain that pleased him, and he asked the jeweller to name his price for the two ornaments. The old man urged him to inspect the remarkable fittings on several old-fashioned saddles studded with semi-precious stones, but he replied that as a merchant's son he had never had much to do with horses, indeed could not even ride and would get no pleasure from saddles old or new; and paying for what he had purchased with a gold piece and a few silver coins, he showed some impatience to be leaving the shop. The old man did not say another word, and while he was selecting a beautiful piece of tissue paper and wrapping up the chain and beryl ornaments separately, the merchant's son chanced to go up to the single low latticed window and look out. He observed a very well-kept vegetable garden, evidently belonging to the neighbouring house, with two greenhouses and a high wall along the boundary. He at once wanted to inspect the greenhouses, and asked the jeweller how he could reach them.

The jeweller handed him his two packages and led him through a side room into the yard, which was connected to the neighbouring garden by a small trellised iron gate. Here the jeweller stopped and knocked at the gate with an iron clapper. But since all remained quite silent in the garden and nobody stirred in the neighbouring house either, he urged the merchant's son to go and have a look at the hothouses, and if he were bothered by anyone to refer to him, as he knew the owner of the garden well. Then reaching through the bars he opened the gate. The merchant's son immediately walked along the wall to the nearest greenhouse, and on entering found such a profusion of rare and remarkable narcissi, anemones, and other exotic plants quite unfamiliar to him, that it was a long while before he had gazed his fill. At last, however, he looked up and became aware that without his noticing the sun had gone down behind the houses. Now he did not want to remain in a strange unattended garden any longer, but thought he would just take a look through the windows of the second greenhouse from outside and then leave. As he was walking along its glass walls peeping in, he suddenly had a severe fright and started back. Someone was watching him with face against the panes. A moment later he grew calmer, realising that it was a child, a girl four years old at most, whose white dress and pale face were pressed against the glass. But then when he looked closer, he had another fright, and felt an unpleasant spasm of horror run down his neck, and a gradual constriction of his throat and chest. For the motionless child fixing him with an angry stare in some inexplicable way resembled the fifteen-year-old girl in his own home. Everything was the same, the fair eyebrows, the fine quivering nostrils, the thin lips; and like the other girl, this child hunched one shoulder slightly. Everything was the same, except that in this child it all produced an expression that quite terrified him. He had no idea why he should feel this nameless fear. All he knew was that he could not bear to turn round and know that behind him this face would be staring through the panes.

In trepidation he hurried towards the greenhouse door, intent

on entering; the door was closed, bolted on the outside; hastily
he bent down low to reach the bolt, thrust it back with such
violence he wrenched his little finger painfully, and advanced
towards the child almost at a run. The child came towards him
and without saying a word braced herself against his knees and,
pushing with her weak little hands, tried to drive him out. He
narrowly avoided stepping on her. But his fear receded now that
he was close to her. He bent over the child's face, which was
quite pale, her eyes trembling with anger and hatred, while her
lower teeth were clenched against her upper lip in uncanny fury.
His fear left him for a moment as he stroked the girl's short fine
hair. But instantly he recalled the hair of the girl at home, which
he had once touched as she lay deathly pale with eyes closed in
her bed, and at once a shiver again ran down his spine and he
withdrew his hand. By now she had given up her attempt to push
him out. She stepped back a few paces and stared straight ahead.
He found the sight of her frail doll's body inside her little white
dress, and her contemptuous, ghastly pale child's face almost
intolerable. He was so filled with horror that he felt a sharp pain
in his throat and temples when his hand touched something cold
inside his pocket. It was a few silver coins. He took them out,
bent down to the child and gave them to her, since they jingled
and were nice and shiny. The child took them and flung them at
his feet, where they disappeared down a crack in the floor-boards,
which rested on a timber frame. Then she turned her back on
him and slowly walked away. For a while he stood motionless, his
heart palpitating with fear lest she should come back and peer
through the panes at him from outside. He would have liked to
leave at once, but it seemed better to let some time elapse so that
the child could leave the garden first. It was now no longer quite
light in the greenhouse, and the shapes of the plants began to
appear strange. Some distance away, dark mysteriously threatening branches loomed up disturbingly out of the gloom, and
behind them there was a glimmer of something white, as though
the child were standing there. On a shelf stood a row of earthenware flowerpots with waxy flowers. To help pass the time he

counted the flowers, which were too stiff to be like living flowers and had something mask-like about them: insidious masks with the eye-holes run together. When he had finished he went to the door and tried to get out. The door would not yield: the child had bolted it on the outside. He felt like screaming but was afraid of the sound of his own voice. He beat against the panes with his fists. The garden and the house remained deathly quiet. Behind him something flitted through the branches with a rustling sound. He told himself it was only leaves falling, shaken loose by his disturbance of the sultry air. Despite this he stopped his banging and peered through the tangle of trees and climbing plants in the semi-darkness. Then against the dim back wall he glimpsed what appeared to be a rectangle of darker lines. He crept towards it, by now unconcerned that he was trampling over flowerpots and that the tall slender stems and palm fronds were closing ghost-like over and behind him. The rectangle of darker lines was the outline of a door and when he pushed, it yielded. The fresh air swept over his face: behind him he could hear the crushed stems and compressed leaves rustling softly in righting themselves as if after a storm.

He was standing in a narrow walled lane; above him he could see the open sky, and the walls on either side scarcely exceeded a man's height. But after fifteen paces or so the lane was bricked up and he thought he was trapped again. Irresolutely he continued on. A shoulder-width opening had been made in the wall on his right, and from there a board stretched across thin air to a platform opposite; this was bounded on the near side by a low iron railing and on two other sides by the backs of tall inhabited houses. Where the board rested like a gang-plank against the edge of the platform, there was a little gate in the railing.

So impatient was the merchant's son to escape the dominion of his fear that he immediately placed first one foot, then the other on the board, and fixing his gaze firmly on the opposite side, began to walk across. But unfortunately, he now became aware that he was suspended over a walled moat several storeys deep; his soles and knee joints felt paralysed by fear and helplessness, and his whole body reeling, he sensed the proximity of death. He knelt down and closed his eyes, then groped forward with his arms until he hit against the bars of the railing. He grabbed them firmly but they gave way, and with a low creak that sounded like the kiss of death and cut him to the quick, the gate to which he was clinging swung towards him – towards the abyss. With a feeling of utter exhaustion and despair he could picture in advance how the smooth iron bars would slip from his fingers, a child's fingers as it seemed to him, and he would hurtle down and be dashed against the wall. But the slow outward movement of the gate was arrested before he lost his footing on the board, and with one leap he flung his trembling body through the gap and onto firm ground.

He did not feel in the least exultant; without looking round, and with an obscure feeling resembling hatred at the senselessness of all these torments, he entered one of the houses and descending the neglected stairs stepped out into an ugly common street. By this stage he was extremely tired and depressed and could think of nothing that seemed worth rejoicing over. In a strange way everything had abandoned him, and feeling utterly empty and forsaken by life, he walked down the street and then the next one and the next. He took a direction he knew would lead him back to the wealthy part of town, where he would be able to find lodging for the night. He was yearning for bed. With childish longing he recalled the beauty of his own wide bed, and remembered the beds the great king from the past had erected for himself and his companions when they held nuptials with the daughters of the subjugated kings: a gold bed for himself, and silver for the others, each supported by griffins and winged oxen. Meanwhile he had come to the low buildings where the soldiers lived. He paid no attention to them. A few soldiers with sallow faces and sad eyes were sitting at a barred window and called something out to him. At this he raised his head and breathed in the stale odour coming from their room, an extraordinarily oppressive smell. He could not make out what they wanted. But since they had roused him from his heedless wandering he now looked into the courtyard as he went by the entrance. The courtyard was very large and sad, and as it was dusk it appeared larger and sadder still. There were very few people about and the surrounding buildings were low and a dirty yellow colour. All this made the yard seem even larger and more desolate. In one spot about twenty horses were tethered in a straight line; in front of each horse, a soldier in stable overalls of coarse cloth was on his knees washing its hooves. From a doorway at the very far end of the courtyard many more soldiers in similar coarse garments were emerging in double file. They walked slowly, with shuffling steps, and carried heavy sacks on their shoulders. Only when they came nearer did he see that the open sacks they were silently lugging were filled with bread. He watched as they slowly vanished through another doorway, trudging off as if under some ugly insidious burden, carrying their bread in sacks like those clothing the sadness of their bodies.

Then he went over to the soldiers who were on their knees in front of the horses washing their hooves. They too looked alike and resembled the soldiers at the window and those who had been carrying the bread. They must have been recruited from neighbouring villages. And they too scarcely spoke a word to one another. Since they found it difficult to hold their horses' forelegs, their heads swayed and their tired sallow faces bent and rose as if in a strong wind. The heads of most of the horses were ugly and had a vicious expression, with ears laid back and upper lip withdrawn to reveal the eye-teeth. Most of them also had angry rolling eyes and a strange impatient and contemptuous way of blowing air out through distended nostrils. The last horse in the row was especially strong and ugly. As the man knelt before it rubbing its hoof dry, it was trying to sink its large teeth into his shoulder. The man had such hollow cheeks and such a deathly sad expression in his tired eyes that the merchant's son was overwhelmed by a deep bitter feeling of compassion. He wanted to cheer the wretched fellow up, at least for the moment, with a gift, and he reached into his pocket for some silver coins. Not finding any he remembered how he had tried to give the last of them to the child in the greenhouse, and how she had scattered them at his feet with that wicked look. He began to hunt for a gold coin instead, having put seven or eight into his pocket for the journey.

At that moment the horse turned its head and looked at him with ears laid back maliciously, its rolling eyes appearing all the more wild and wicked because of a white patch running across its ugly head just at the level of its eyes. At this sight a long-forgotten human face flashed through his mind. However hard he might have tried at any other time to recall that person's features, he would not have been able to, but now there they were. The memory that came with the face, however, was not so distinct. All he knew was that it went back to when he was twelve years old, to a time which was somehow associated in his mind with the sweet smell of warm peeled almonds.

And he knew that it was the contorted face of an ugly poverty-stricken man he had seen only once in his father's shop. And that the face was contorted with fear because people were threatening him, because he had a large gold coin and would not say where he had come by it.

As the face faded once again, his fingers continued to search in the folds of his clothes, but when a sudden vague thought made him hesitate, he pulled his hand out irresolutely and in doing so flung the piece of jewellery with the beryl wrapped in tissue paper under the legs of the horse. He bent down, the horse kicked him sideways in the groin with all its might, and he fell over on his back. He groaned aloud, drew up his knees and kept beating the ground with his heels. A few of the soldiers stood up and lifted him by the shoulders and behind the knees. He was conscious of their clothes, the same stale wretched smell that had come from the room on the street earlier, and tried to remember where he had smelt it before, long, long ago; and as he did so he lost consciousness. They carried him up a low flight of steps, through a long half-dark passage to one of their rooms, and laid him on a low iron bed. Then they searched his clothes, took the little chain and the seven gold coins and eventually, stirred to pity by his incessant groaning, went to fetch one of their surgeons.

After a time he opened his eyes and became conscious of his agonising pain. But being alone in this comfortless room frightened and worried him even more. With an effort he turned his eyes in their aching sockets towards the wall, and on a shelf noticed three loaves of the same kind of bread the soldiers had been carrying across the courtyard.

Otherwise there was nothing in the room except the low hard beds and the smell of the dry reeds with which the mattresses were stuffed, and then that other stale wretched odour.

For a while he was completely preoccupied by his pain, and the stifling mortal terror compared with which the pain was a relief. Then for a moment he managed to forget his mortal fear and to reflect on how all this had come about.

Then he felt a different kind of fear, less oppressive but more pervasive, a fear which he was not feeling for the first time, but which he now experienced as something he had overcome. And he clenched his fists and cursed his servants, who had driven him to his death – his manservant to the city, the old woman into the jeweller's shop, the girl into the back room and the child by means of her treacherous double into the greenhouse, from where he then found himself staggering up hideous steps and over bridges and collapsing beneath the horse's hooves. Then he started whimpering like a child, not out of pain but out of sorrow, and his teeth chattered.

He looked back over his life with great bitterness and disavowed everything that he had cherished. He hated his untimely death so much that he hated his life for having led him to it. The wild inner frenzy consumed his last remaining strength. He became dizzy and again fell into a delirious wretched sleep for a while. Then he awoke and tried to scream because he was still alone, but his voice gave out. Finally he vomited gall, then blood, and died, his features distorted, his lips so mangled that his teeth and gums were exposed, giving him an alien, evil expression.

A Cavalry Tale

ON 22 JULY 1848, just before six o'clock in the morning, a raiding party of a hundred and seven men of the Second Squadron, the Wallmoden Cuirassiers, under the command of Captain Baron Rofrano, left its quarters in San Alessandro and rode towards Milan. Over the bright open landscape lay an indescribable tranquillity; from the summits of the distant mountains morning clouds ascended into the radiant sky like silent trails of smoke; the maize stood motionless, and between clumps of trees that looked freshly washed houses and churches gleamed. The detachment had advanced scarcely a mile or so beyond its own army's foremost picket when there was a flash of fire among the maizefields and the vanguard reported enemy infantry. The squadron drew up in attack formation beside the road, then, with the characteristically loud, almost miaowing whine of bullets passing overhead, charged across the fields and routed a party of variously armed men, scattering them like quails. They belonged to the Manaras Legion and wore outlandish head-dress. The prisoners were handed over to a corporal and eight troopers and dispatched to the rear. The vanguard reported suspicious figures in front of a fine villa, the approach to which was flanked by ancient cypresses. The sergeant, Anton Lerch, dismounted, picked twelve men armed with carbines, surrounded the windows and captured eighteen students of the Pisan Legion, all well-bred, handsome young men with white hands and near shoulder-length hair. Half an hour later the squadron detained a man in Bergamasque costume who aroused suspicion by his excessively innocent and unassuming demeanour as he walked past. Sewn into the lining of his coat the man was carrying vital details of plans regarding the setting up of a corps of volunteers in Giudicaria and their intended joint action with the Piedmontese Army. Around ten o'clock that morning a herd of cattle fell into the hands of the detachment. Immediately a strong enemy force confronted them and fired on the forward troops from behind a churchyard wall. Lieutenant Count Trautsohn's spearhead troop leaped over the low wall and lashed out with their sabres at the bewildered enemy among the graves, a large number of whom escaped into the church and from there through the vestry into thick woodland. The twenty-seven new prisoners identified themselves as a Neapolitan volunteer corps under papal officers. The squadron lost one man killed. A party consisting of private Wotrubek and dragoons Holl and Haindl, riding round the wood, captured a light howitzer drawn by two plough-horses, laying about the escort with their swords and seizing the horses by the bridle and turning them round. Private Wotrubek, being slightly wounded, was sent back to headquarters to report on the successful engagements and other good news thus far, and the prisoners were also transported to the rear, but the howitzer accompanied the squadron which, less the rear-bound detachments, still numbered seventy-eight cavalrymen.

Since according to the unanimous testimony of the various prisoners the city of Milan had been completely abandoned by both regular and irregular enemy troops, and stripped of all ordnance and military supplies, the captain could not deny himself or the squadron the opportunity of riding into this large and beautiful city lying defenceless before them. Amid the noon pealing of bells, with four blaring trumpets sounding the general advance into the steely brilliance of the sky, rattling a thousand gleaming panes mirrored in seventy-eight cuirasses and as many raised bare swords; with streets to right and left filling up like a disturbed ant-heap with astonished faces, frightened cursing figures vanishing through doorways, drowsy shutters flinging open to reveal pretty bare-armed strangers; past San Babila, San Fedele and San Carlo, past the world-famous marble cathedral, past San Satiro, San Giorgio, San Lorenzo, San Eustorgio, all their ancient bronze doors opening to afford glimpses of silver saints and starry-eyed brocaded women amid candlelight and incense; always anticipating shots from a thousand attics, dark archways and squalid shops, but greeted instead by stripling girls and boys showing their white teeth and dusky hair; surveying all this from the height of their trotting chargers, their eyes sparkling behind masks of dust and blood; in at the Porta Venezia and out again at the Porta Ticinese – thus rode the splendid squadron through Milan.

Not far from the last-mentioned city gate and the slope of a fort planted with fine plane trees, Sergeant Anton Lerch thought he recognised the face of a woman he knew at the ground-floor window of a newly-built bright yellow house. Curiosity prompted him to turn in his saddle, and since just then a slight stiffness in his horse's gait made him suspect a pebble might have lodged under one of its front shoes, and since too he was riding at the rear of the squadron and could fall out without any disruption, he decided to dismount, having first manoeuvred the fore part of his horse into the courtyard of the house. Scarcely had he raised the second of the bay's white forefetlocks to examine the hoof when a house door near the front of the yard opened and the voluptuous figure of a still youngish woman appeared, her dressing-gown in some disorder, while behind her the sergeant glimpsed a bright room with garden windows set off by little pots of basil and red pelargonia, a mahogany chest and a mythological group in biscuit porcelain, his keen eye instantly taking in the reflection of the opposite wall in a pier-glass, filled by a great white bed and a concealed door through which a stout, clean-shaven older man was just retreating.

And as the sergeant recalled the woman's name along with a host of other details – that she was the widow or divorced wife of a Croatian paymaster-sergeant, how nine or ten years ago in Vienna he and a comrade who was at the time her lover had often spent the evening and half the night together in her company – his eyes sought to recapture her former slender succulent figure beneath her present fullness. But the woman now standing before him smiled at him in a half-fawning, Slavic way that sent the blood surging through his powerful neck and up behind his eyes, while her somewhat affected manner of addressing him, along with her dressing-gown and the room-furnishings, had an intimidating effect on him. But in a trice, as he languidly watched a large fly crawling over the woman's hair-comb, outwardly concerned with nothing more than swiftly placing his hand on her white, warm yet cool nape to chase away the fly, he was suffused from head to foot with the consciousness of today's success in battle and other vicissitudes of fortune, and with his powerful hand drew her head toward him and said: 'Vuic,' – for ten years her name had certainly not passed his lips, and he had forgotten her Christian name completely – 'in a week we will occupy the city, and then this,' pointing to the half-open door of the room, 'will be my billet.' Here he heard doors inside the house being slammed repeatedly, and sensing his horse urging him away, first by a mute tugging at the reins, then by its loud neighing for its companions, he mounted and trotted off after the squadron, taking with him no firmer reply from Vuic than an embarrassed laugh and shrug of the shoulders. But the words he had spoken were an assertion of his power. Riding to one side of the column, his brisk pace much slackened under the heavy metallic glare of the sky, his vision obscured by the accompanying dust cloud, the sergeant became more and more absorbed in thoughts of the room with the mahogany furniture and the pots of basil, of a civilian atmosphere in which the martial spirit still shone through, an atmosphere of ease and gratifying dominion without military duties, an existence in house-slippers with the hilt of his sabre poking through the left pocket of his dressing-gown. And the stout, clean-shaven man who had disappeared through the concealed door, a cross between priest and pensioned-off valet, played an important role in this whole fantasy, almost more so than the fine broad bed and Vuic's delicate white skin. One moment the clean-shaven fellow assumed the part of a confidential, somewhat obsequious friend, who related court gossip and brought him capons and tobacco; the next he was being pressed against the wall and forced to pay hush-money, had his finger in all sorts of intrigues, was a Piedmontese agent, a cook in papal service, a procurer, or the owner of suspect houses with shady garden rooms for political meetings, whereupon he grew into a spongy giant into whose body bungholes could be bored in twenty different places and gold siphoned off instead of blood.

During the afternoon the raiding party encountered nothing new, and there was little to inhibit the sergeant's reveries. But a thirst for unexpected windfalls had been aroused within him, for bonuses, for ducats suddenly filling his pocket. And the anticipation of his first entry into the room with the mahogany furniture was the splinter in the flesh around which all these desires and cravings swelled.

When towards evening the raiding party, with horses fed and adequately rested, was advancing in an arc towards Lodi and the Adda bridge, where contact with the enemy could confidently be expected, the sergeant noticed a village with a half-dilapidated belfry lying off the road in a darkening hollow which looked to him temptingly suspicious, so beckoning privates Holl and Scarmolin to follow, he turned aside from the direction of the squadron's march, hoping, so excited was his imagination, to surprise an enemy general with inadequate protection in the village and attack him, or in some other way to earn a quite exceptional reward. Reaching this wretched, apparently deserted hole, he ordered his men to ride round the outside of the houses, Scarmolin to the left and Holl to the right, while he himself with pistol drawn set off at a gallop down the village street; but soon, feeling hard stone paving underfoot on which slippery grease appeared to have been spilled, he had to rein in his horse. The village was deathly still; not a child, not a bird, not a breath of air. To right and left stood squalid little houses with mortar crumbling from the walls; in places on the bare bricks obscene drawings had been made in charcoal; peering in between exposed doorposts, here and there the sergeant saw a decrepit half-naked

figure slouching on a bed or dragging across a room as if on
dislocated hips. His horse advanced with difficulty, thrusting
with its hind legs as though they were of lead. As he turned in
the saddle and bent to check a rear shoe, he heard footsteps shuffling out from one of the houses, and when he straightened up he
saw walking just in front of his horse a female figure whose face
he could not see. She was only half-dressed; her dirty, torn skirt
of patterned silk trailed in the gutter, and her stockingless feet
were thrust into dirty slippers; she walked so close to the horse
that the breath from its nostrils stirred the mass of greasy curls
falling over her bare neck from beneath an old straw hat; and yet
she did not increase her pace or get out of the cavalryman's way.
From a doorway on the left two bleeding rats, their teeth locked
in each other's flesh, rolled into the middle of the road, the one
underneath squealing so pitiably that the sergeant's horse held
back and, with head averted and breathing audibly, stared at the
ground. Pressure from his thighs got it moving again, but by
now the woman had disappeared through a doorway without the
sergeant's having caught sight of her face. A dog ran hurriedly
out of the next house, its head held high, dropped a bone in the
middle of the road and tried to bury it in a crack between the
paving stones. It was a dirty white bitch with hanging teats; it
scratched the earth with fiendish concentration, then seized the
bone in its teeth and carried it on a little further. While it was
beginning to scratch afresh, three more dogs suddenly appeared;
two were very young with soft bones and flabby skin; without
barking or being capable of biting they dragged each other about
by the flews with their blunt teeth. The other dog that had come
with them was a yellowish whippet with such a swollen belly that
it could only move forward very slowly on its skinny legs. In
relation to its distended body, taut as a drum, its head looked far
too small; there was an expression of terrible anguish in its restless little eyes. Suddenly two more dogs bounded up: a lean
white one, ravenous and extremely ugly, with black mucus
running from its inflamed eyes, and a long-legged mongrel
dachshund. The latter raised its head and gazed at the sergeant.

It must have been very old. Its eyes were infinitely sad and weary. The bitch, however, scurried stupidly back and forth in front of the rider; the two young dogs snapped silently with their soft mouths at the horse's fetlocks, and the whippet dragged its horrible body along straight in front of its hooves. The bay could not take another step. But when the sergeant tried to fire at one of the animals and his pistol jammed, he set both spurs to his horse and clattered away over the stone paving. After a few steps, however, he was forced to rein his horse in sharply. For here the way was blocked by a cow which a boy was dragging by a taut rope to the shambles. But the cow, recoiling at the reek of blood and the fresh skin of a black calf nailed to the doorpost, braced its legs to resist, sucking in the red evening dust through dilated nostrils, and before the boy who was beating and tugging it could get it across the road, with a piteous look snatched one last mouthful of hay from the bundle the sergeant had tied in front of his saddle. Now he had left the last house in the village behind, and riding between two low crumbling walls, he could make out the course of the road on the other side of an old single-arched stone bridge spanning an apparently dry ditch, but he felt such an indescribable heaviness in his horse's gait, such a sense of arrested motion, that every foot of the walls to left and right, indeed every millipede and woodlouse sheltering there, seemed to pass laboriously before his eyes, and he felt he had spent an immeasurable time riding through this revolting village. Just then, as a heavy whining sigh came from his horse's chest, a highly unusual noise which he failed to recognise immediately and the cause of which he sought first above him, then around him and finally in the distance, he noticed a cavalryman from his own regiment approaching him from beyond the stone bridge, as it happened as far from the bridge on the other side as he was on this, and furthermore a sergeant, and furthermore astride a bay with white front fetlocks. Since he knew full well that there was no such horse in the entire squadron other than the one on which he was seated at that moment, but still could not recognise the other rider's face, he impatiently spurred his horse on to a rapid trot, at which the other cavalryman increased his pace by exactly the same amount, so that only a stone's throw now lay between them, whereupon as the two horses, each from its own side, stepped onto the bridge at the same moment with the same white foreleg, the sergeant stared aghast at this apparition in which he suddenly recognised himself, and frantically reining in his horse he raised his right hand with fingers splayed to ward the creature off, at which the figure, likewise reining in and lifting its right hand, was suddenly no longer there and privates Holl and Scarmolin appeared with nonchalant faces to the right and left up out of the dry ditch, just as, not far off across the meadow, the squadron's trumpets loudly sounded the attack. Galloping at full tilt up a slope, the sergeant saw the squadron moving at a gallop towards a copse, from which enemy cavalry armed with lances hastily debouched. Gathering the four loose reins in his left hand and binding the wrist-thong round his right, he saw the fourth troop separate from the squadron and proceed more slowly, but already he was galloping over the rumbling ground amid a strong smell of dust into the thick of the enemy, and as he struck out at a blue arm holding a lance, he caught a glimpse of the captain's face close by him, with wide staring eyes and fiercely bared teeth; then suddenly finding himself wedged in among a throng of hostile faces and enemy colours, he plunged into a sea of waving swords, struck the nearest man in the throat and knocked him from his horse, saw private Scarmolin beside him gleefully hewing off the fingers of a hand holding the reins and burying his sabre deep in the horse's neck, felt the mêlée thin out, and was suddenly alone on the bank of a small stream behind an enemy officer on an iron-grey horse. The officer tried to get across the stream but the horse refused the jump. The officer swung his horse round and turned a very young pale face and the muzzle of his pistol towards the sergeant at the very moment that a sabre struck him in the mouth, in the sharp tip of which the full weight of a galloping horse was concentrated. The sergeant wrenched his sabre free and snatched up the reins just where the officer's fingers had released them as he toppled from the iron grey, which lifted its feet over its dying master as lightly and daintily as a deer.

As the sergeant rode back with the fine horse he had captured, the sun going down in a dense haze cast an immense red glow over the meadow. Even in places where there were no hoof marks there seemed to be whole pools of blood. The crimson radiance was reflected in the white uniforms and laughing faces, in the cuirasses and saddlecloths that glowed and sparkled, and above all in three small fig trees on the soft leaves of which the troopers had jubilantly wiped the blood from the grooves of their swords. To one side of the blood-stained trees stood the captain and beside him the squadron trumpeter, who raised a trumpet that might have been dipped in crimson juice to his lips and sounded the rally. The sergeant rode from troop to troop and found that the squadron had not lost one man but had captured nine horses. He rode up to the captain and made his report, still with the iron grey beside him which capered and sniffed the air like the fine vain young horse it was. The captain listened to the report with only half an ear. He beckoned Lieutenant Count Trautsohn over to him, who immediately dismounted and with six cuiras-siers who had likewise dismounted, unyoked the captured light howitzer behind the assembled squadron, ordered the gun to be towed to one side by the six men and dumped into a small swamp formed by the stream, then remounted, and after driving off the two now redundant plough-horses with the flat of his sword, silently resumed his place in front of the first troop. In the mean-time the squadron, lined up in two ranks, although not exactly restless, was in quite an unusual mood, perhaps attributable to the excitement of having been in four successful actions on one day, which manifested itself in sporadic outbursts of half-suppressed laughter and remarks exchanged in undertones. Nor were the horses less restive, especially where the captured horses had been mingled with the rest. After such a run of successes they all seemed to find the space they were drawn up in too confining, and inwardly these victorious cavalrymen felt the urge to advance in a loose horde upon some new enemy, lay about them and capture further horses. At this moment Captain Baron Rofrano rode up to the front of his squadron and, raising the heavy lids of his rather sleepy blue eyes, audibly but without raising his voice gave the command: 'Release the captured horses!' The squadron stood still as death. Only the iron-grey beside the sergeant stretched out its neck and with its nostrils almost touched the forehead of the horse on which the captain was seated. The captain sheathed his sabre, drew one of his pistols from its holster and, wiping a speck of dust from the gleaming barrel with the back of his bridle hand, repeated the command in a slightly louder voice and immediately began counting, 'one', 'two'. After counting 'two' he fixed his veiled eyes on the sergeant, who sat motionless before him in the saddle staring steadily into the captain's face. While Anton Lerch's unwavering gaze, in which fleetingly something oppressed and currish flickered, might have seemed to contain an air of devoted reliability born of many years of service, his conscious mind hardly registered the extraordinary tenseness of the moment, being overwhelmed with innumerable images of exotic ease, and suddenly, from depths of his being completely unfamiliar to him, a bestial rage arose against the man before him who wanted to take away his horse, a terrible fury against the face, the voice, the bearing of this man, such as can only develop in some mysterious way through long years of living in close familiarity. Whether something similar was going on inside the captain, or whether the contagious dangers lurking in all critical situations seemed to him to be concentrated in this moment of mute insubordination, must remain in doubt. He raised his arm in a nonchalant, almost affected manner, and as he curled his upper lip contemptuously and counted 'three' the shot rang out and the sergeant lurched forward, hit in the head, his upper body falling onto his horse's neck then down to the ground between the bay and the iron-grey. Even before he hit the earth, all the non-commissioned officers and men rid themselves of their captured horses with a kick or a tug on the reins, and the captain, calmly returning his pistol to its holster, was once again able to lead the squadron, still reeling from this lightning blow, against the enemy, who in the dim twilight appeared to be rallying in the distance. The enemy, however, declined battle, and soon afterwards the detachment reached the southern outpost positions of its own army without further incident.

Marshal de Bassompierre's Adventure

A T A CERTAIN PERIOD in my life my duties were such that fairly regularly, several times a week, I would cross over the Petit Pont (for the Pont Neuf had not as yet been built) at exactly the same hour, and so would usually be recognised and greeted by several craftsmen and others from among the common people, but most conspicuously by a very pretty tradeswoman whose shop sign bore two angels, and who as often as I passed by during those five or six months would bow deeply and gaze after me until I was out of sight. Struck by her behaviour, I would return her gaze and courteously acknowledge her. Once in late winter when, riding from Fontainebleau to Paris, I again crossed the Petit Pont, she came to the door of her shop and said to me as I rode past: 'Your humble servant, my Lord!' I greeted her in turn, and looking round from time to time, saw that she was craning forward so as to watch me for as long as possible. I had a servant and a postilion in train, whom I intended to send back to Fontainebleau that same evening with letters to certain ladies. I ordered the servant to dismount and go up to the young woman, and to tell her on my behalf that I had noticed her habit of gazing at me and greeting me and that if she wished to make my closer acquaintance, I would meet her wherever she proposed.

She replied to the servant that he could not have brought her a more welcome message and she would meet me wherever I requested.

As we rode on, I asked the servant whether he happened to know of a place where the woman and I might meet. He replied that he would take her to the house of a certain go-between;

but being an extremely responsible and conscientious fellow, this servant William from Courtrai, he immediately added that since the plague had broken out in various places, and not only people from the lower dirt-ridden orders but a doctor and a prebendary had already died from it, he would advise me to have mattresses, quilts and sheets brought over from my house. I accepted the proposal and he promised to make up a comfortable bed for me. Before dismounting I added that he should bring along a proper washbasin, a small phial with aromatic essence, and some apples and pastries; he should also see to it that the room was thoroughly heated, for it was so cold my feet had frozen in the stirrups, and the sky was full of looming snowclouds.

That evening I made my way to the house arranged and found a very beautiful woman of about twenty sitting on the bed, while the go-between, her head and bent back draped in a black shawl, was talking to her eagerly. The door was ajar and large fresh logs were blazing noisily in the fireplace: they had not heard me coming and I paused for a moment at the door. The young woman gazed calmly and wide-eyed at the flames; and as she tossed her head, as if to put as much distance as possible between herself and the revolting crone, some of her heavy auburn hair escaped from under the little night bonnet she was wearing, curling naturally into ringlets and falling over her nightshirt between her breasts and shoulders. In addition she was wearing a short green woollen undergarment and slippers. I must have betrayed my presence by some sound: flinging her head round, she turned her face towards me, and the extreme tenseness of her features would have given her an almost wild expression but for the aura of surrender radiating from her wide eyes and flickering from her speechless mouth like an invisible flame. I found her extraordinarily attractive, and in a trice the old crone was out of the room and I beside my lady friend. When in the first intoxication of unexpected possession I ventured certain liberties, she withdrew from me with a lively determination in her look and deeply resonant voice that defies description. But the very next moment I found myself in the embrace of a woman who clung to me as fervently and persistently with her upturned gaze as with her lips and arms; or again, it was as if she wished to speak, but her lips, throbbing with kisses, would form no words, her trembling throat articulate no sound beyond a broken sob.

Now I had spent a large part of that day on horseback riding along frosty highways, and then attended a very irksome and heated meeting in the king's antechamber, after which, to drown my foul mood, I had both drunk a fair amount and done some vigorous sparring with the broadsword; so that in the middle of this delightful and mysterious adventure, as I lay with her arms about my neck and strands of her fragrant hair strewn over me, I was suddenly so overcome by extreme fatigue, verging on stupor, that I could no longer recall how I came to be in that particular room, indeed for a moment confused the woman whose heart beat so close to mine with a completely different person from the past, and almost at once fell fast asleep.

When I awoke, it was still the dead of night, but I sensed at once that my lady friend was no longer by my side. I raised my head and by the dim light of the settling embers could see that she was standing at the window: she had pushed open one of the shutters and was looking out through the gap. Then she turned round, noticed that I was awake, and called out (I can still see her raising her left hand to her cheek and sweeping her hair back over her shoulder as she spoke): 'It's nowhere near daylight, nowhere near!' Only now did I really appreciate how tall and beautiful she was, and could hardly wait for the moment when, with a few calm strides, the reddish firelight flickering over her lovely feet, she would again be by my side. First however she went over to the hearth, bent down, took the last heavy log in her gleaming naked arms and quickly threw it on the fire. Then she turned round, her face in the firelight radiant with joy, and picking up an apple from the table as she passed, lay down beside me, her limbs still aglow with the fire's fresh warmth which then quickly dissipated, only to be replaced by more ardent flames from within as, clasping me with her right arm, she offered the cool already tasted fruit and her cheeks, lips and eyes to my eager mouth.

The last log in the hearth burned more brightly than the others. Flaring up, it sucked in the flames and then released them so that they blazed forth vigorously, and the firelight swept over us like a wave breaking against the wall, suddenly raising our embracing shadows and letting them sink back again. Repeatedly the stout log spluttered, nurturing ever new tongues of flame which leapt upwards and dispelled the oppressive darkness with scattered sheaves of reddish light. Then suddenly the flames subsided and a chill breath of air opened the shutter softly, like a hand, to reveal the pale abhorrent dawn.

We sat up and became aware that it was already day. But the scene out there did not resemble day. It did not resemble the awakening of the world. What lay outside did not look like a street. No detail could be made out: it was a colourless, feature-less wasteland in which timeless ghosts might roam. From some-where far away, as if from the realm of memory, a church clock struck, and a cold damp wind, which belonged to no hour, blew in ever more fiercely, so that we clung shivering to one another. She leaned back and fixed her eyes on my face with great inten-sity; her throat contracted and something welled up inside her and trembled on her lips – not quite a word, or a sigh, or a kiss, but something unborn resembling all three. Moment by moment it was growing lighter and the complex agitated expression on her face more eloquent; then suddenly, outside, shuffling steps and voices passed so close by the window that she ducked and turned her face towards the wall. Two men were walking past and for an instant light penetrated into the room from a little lantern one of them was carrying; the other was pushing a barrow with a wheel that groaned and clattered. When they had passed, I got up, closed the shutter and lit a lamp. There lay the half-eaten apple: we finished it together, and then I asked her whether I might see her again, as I would not be leaving until Sunday. This had been the night of Thursday to Friday.

She replied that she desired this even more than I did, but that if I were not staying for the whole of Sunday it would be impossible; she could only see me again on the night of Sunday to Monday.

Several obstacles occurred to me at first and I raised a few objections, to all of which she listened in silence, with a pained enquiring look, while her face hardened and darkened almost uncannily. Then I promised to stay all Sunday, and added that I would find my way to the same place on Sunday evening. At this she looked at me steadily and in a harsh broken voice replied: 'I'm well aware of having come to a house of shame for your sake; but I did so of my own free will, because I *wanted* to be with you, because I would have agreed to *any* conditions. But now I would regard myself as the lowest street-walker if I could bring myself to come back here a second time. I did this for your sake, because to me you are the man you are, because you are Bassompierre, because you are the only person in the world whose presence could make this house an honourable place to me!' She said 'house', but for a moment it seemed as if a more contemptuous term were on the tip of her tongue, and as she uttered the word she cast such a withering look at the four walls, the bed, the quilt that had slithered to the floor, that all these ugly, sordid things seemed to start and retreat cowering before her, making the wretched room look larger for a moment.

Then in an indescribably gentle and dignified voice she added: 'May I die a miserable death if I have ever belonged to anyone else except my husband and yourself, or if I should ever desire anyone else on earth!', and standing with her lips half-open, life-breathing and a little pursed, she seemed to await some kind of answer, some affirmation of my faith in her; but then evidently not reading in my face what she desired, her expectant searching gaze grew clouded, her eyelashes began to tremble, and suddenly she was at the window with her back turned to me, her forehead pressed with all her might against the shutter, and her whole body so convulsed with silent yet frighteningly violent sobs that the words died on my lips and I did not dare to touch her. Finally I grasped her hand as it hung lifeless by her side, and with the most persuasive words that occurred to me at that moment, I at length succeeded in so far appeasing her that she again turned her tear-drenched face towards me, then suddenly a smile burst forth like sunlight from her eyes and lips, dispelling all trace of tears in a moment and flooding her whole face with radiance.

Now as she began to talk to me again, the most delightful game developed, in which she played endless variations on the words: 'You want to see me again? Then I shall let you into my aunt's place!', pronouncing the question in a dozen different ways, now with sweet intensity, now with childishly playful misgiving, and then whispering the answer in my ear as though it were the greatest secret, then tossing it over her shoulder with a pert mouth and a shrug, as though it were the most natural arrangement in the world, and finally, as she clung to me, repeating it coaxingly and laughing in my face. She described the house to me as one might describe the way to a child about to cross the street to the baker's alone for the first time. Then she rose and became serious – her radiant eyes transfixing me with such overwhelming power that I felt they must be capable of mesmerising even a corpse – and continued: 'I shall be expecting you between ten o'clock and midnight, or later even, indeed forever more, and the door downstairs will be unlocked. First you'll come to a little passage, but don't stop there as my aunt's door opens onto it. Then you'll come to a stair-case which will take you to the first floor and that's where I shall be!' And closing her eyes, as though feeling dizzy, she flung back her head, opened her arms and embraced me; then in a trice she was out of my arms and wrapped in her clothes, and looking aloof and earnest, she left the room; for now it was broad daylight.

I made my own arrangements, sent some of my servants on ahead with my chattels, and by the evening of that day felt such intense impatience that soon after the vespers bell I went across the little bridge with my servant William, instructing him however not to bring a light, so as to enable me at least to catch a glimpse of my lady friend in her shop or adjacent living quarters, and perhaps give her some sign of my presence, even though I was not hoping for anything more than the exchange of a few words.

In order not to make myself conspicuous I remained on the bridge and sent my servant on ahead to reconnoitre. He was away quite some time and on his return wore the downcast brooding look that I had come to recognise in this good fellow whenever he had been unable to carry out one of my orders successfully. 'The shop is locked up,' he said, 'and no one seems to be inside. There's not a soul to be seen or heard in the rooms facing the street. The only way into the courtyard is over a high wall, and there's a large dog growling inside. There's a light in one of the front rooms, and you can see in through a crack in the shutters, but I am afraid it's empty.'

In an ill humour I felt like turning back, but then after all decided to stroll slowly past the house again, and my assiduous servant again put his eye to the crack, through which a gleam of light escaped, and whispered that though the woman was not in the room, the husband was. Curious to see this tradesman, whom I could not remember even once having caught sight of in his shop, and whom I imagined to myself alternately as a fat, uncouth fellow and a fragile dry old man, I went up to the window. Inside the well-furnished panelled room I was utterly astonished to see an uncommonly tall and well-built man, at least a head taller than myself, who on turning round revealed a handsome, deeply serious face, a brown beard flecked with silver, and a brow of almost startling nobility, the temples loftier than I had ever seen in a human being before. Although he was quite alone in the room, his expression would change, his lips would move, and pausing now and then as he strode up and down, he seemed to be conversing in imagination with another person: once he moved his arm as if to dismiss an objection with indulgent superiority. Each of his gestures expressed a great languidness and almost contemptuous pride, and I could not help being vividly reminded by his lonely pacing to and fro of the image of a noble prisoner whom in the service of the king I had once been obliged to guard during his incarceration in the castle tower at Blois. This resemblance seemed all the more complete when the man raised his right hand and scrutinised his bent fingers with close care, indeed with gloomy seriousness.

For I had often seen that noble prisoner examine a ring he was very fond of on his right index finger with almost the same gesture. The man in the room now went to the table, placed the water globe in front of the lighted candle and stretched out the fingers of both hands under the circle of light: he seemed to be examining his nails. Then he blew the light out and left the room, leaving me with a dull angry jealous feeling, for my desire for his wife was growing like a spreading fire, nourished by whatever crossed its path, and was thus enhanced in some confusing way by the sight of this unexpected figure, as indeed by every snowflake that, blown by a cold damp wind, stuck melting to my cheeks and eyebrows.

I spent the following day in the most unprofitable way, could not concentrate at all on business matters, bought a horse I didn't really like, attended the Duke of Nemours after dinner and spent some time there at cards and in banal unpleasant conversation, for the talk was of nothing else but the ever stronger hold the plague was taking in the town, and not a word was to be got out of any of these nobles except stories about the rapid incineration of corpses, the straw fires it was necessary to light in the chambers of the dead to consume the noxious vapours, and so on; but the silliest among these people seemed to me the Canon of Chandieu, who though as fat and healthy as ever, could not restrain himself from continually squinting at his fingernails to see if they showed any tell-tale sign of turning blue, the symptom by which the disease usually announced itself.

Finding all this disgusting, I went home early and retired to bed, but could not sleep, and so got dressed again out of sheer impatience, resolving to go over and see my lady friend whatever the cost, even if I had to enter by force with my retainers. I went to the window to waken my servants, but the icy night air brought me to my senses, and I realised that this was the surest way to ruin everything. I threw myself on the bed clothed as I was and at long last fell asleep.

I spent Sunday until evening in much the same way, and reached the designated street far too early, but forced myself to walk up and down a neighbouring street until the clock struck ten. Then I at once found the house she had described to me: the door was unlocked and beyond it were the passage and the stairs. The second door at the head of the stairs was locked, but from beneath it came a narrow streak of light. So she was in there waiting, perhaps standing listening on the inside of the door as I stood outside. I scratched at the door with my nail, then I heard steps within: they seemed to be the cautious hesitant steps of someone walking barefoot. For a time I stood there breathless, then I started knocking; but a man's voice answered, demanding who was there. I shrank back into the darkness of the door frame and kept absolutely quiet. The door remained closed and with the utmost stealth I retreated step by step back down the stairs, slipped out through the passage into the open, and with clenched teeth and throbbing temples, walked up and down several streets seething with impatience. Finally something drove me back to the house again; but I did not want to enter yet, for I felt certain she would get rid of the man, she was bound to succeed, and I would shortly be able to go up to her. The street was narrow; there were no houses on the other side, but instead the garden wall of a monastery; I pressed up close to it and tried to guess which was her window opposite. In one that stood open on the upper floor a light flared up as from a flame and then subsided. I at once imagined the whole scene: just as before, she had thrown a large log onto the fire, just as before she was now standing in the middle of the room, her limbs radiant from the flames, or sitting on the bed listening and waiting. From the door I would see her and the shadow of her neck and shoulders rising and sinking on the wall like a translucent wave. By this stage I was already in the passage, already on the stairs; the door was no longer locked and stood ajar, letting the unsteady light through sideways. I was on the point of reaching for the door handle when I thought I heard footsteps and several people's voices from inside the room. But I didn't want to believe it: I took it for the blood coursing through my neck and temples and the blazing fire. On my previous visit too it had been blazing noisily. Now I grasped the door handle; I had to face the fact that there were people in there – several people. But I no longer cared, because I was absolutely certain that she was in there too, and that as soon as I pushed the door open I should see her, seize her, and with one arm draw her, if necessary out of the hands of others, to my side, even if this then meant hacking a way through the yelling throng for us both with my sword and dagger! The one thing that seemed utterly intolerable was to wait a moment longer.

I pushed the door open – and saw several people in the middle of the empty room burning bed straw, and by the light of the flames illuminating the whole room, scraped walls with the soot from them lying on the floor, and against one wall a table on which two naked bodies were laid out, one very tall with covered head, the other smaller, stretched out next to the wall, while behind them the dark shadows of their forms rose and fell playfully.

I staggered down the stairs out of the house and ran into two grave-diggers: one of them held his little lantern up to my face and asked me what I wanted, the other pushed his groaning, clattering barrow straight for the main door of the house. I drew my sword to keep them at arm's length and hastened home. There I at once drank three or four large glasses of strong wine, and after I had rested, set out the following day for Lorraine.

Every effort I made on my return to find out anything at all about that woman was in vain. I even went back to the shop under the sign of the two angels; but the people who now occupied it did not know who their predecessors had been.

M. de Bassompierre, *Journal de ma vie*, Cologne, 1665;
Goethe, *Entertainments of German Refugees*, 1795

Letter from Lord Chandos

This is a letter which Philip Lord Chandos, younger son of the Earl of Bath, wrote to Francis Bacon, later Lord Verulam and Viscount St Albans, apologising to his friend for having completely abandoned his literary activities.

IT IS GRACIOUS of you, my esteemed friend, to disregard my two years' silence and write to me like this. It is more than gracious of you to express your concern for me, your dismay at the spiritual torpor into which I seem to you to be sinking, with the levity and wit which only great men thoroughly acquainted with yet undaunted by life's dangers can command.

You close with Hippocrates' aphorism 'Qui gravi morbo correpti dolores non sentiunt, iis mens aegrotat',* and observe that I have need of physic not merely to control my sickness, but even more to sharpen my understanding of my inner state of mind. I would like to respond as befits your concern and to be completely open with you, and yet do not know how to go about it. I scarcely know whether I am still the person to whom your much appreciated letter is addressed; am I, at twenty-six, the same person who at nineteen wrote *Second Paris*, *Daphne's Dream*, *Epithalamium*, those pastoral plays intoxicated with the splendour of their own rhetoric, which a heavenly queen and several all too indulgent lords and gentlemen have been

---

*In his *Advancement of Learning* Bacon quotes these lines in Latin with a rough English translation. W. H. S. Jones, in the Loeb edition of *Hippocrates*, translates the Greek original: 'Those who, suffering from a painful affliction of the body, for the most part are unconscious of the pains, are disordered in mind.'

gracious enough to remember? Or again, am I the person who at twenty-three, beneath the stone colonnades of the grand piazza in Venice, discovered within himself configurations of Latin sentences whose intellectual principles and structure inwardly delighted him more than the buildings of Palladio and Sansovino rising from the sea? And if in other respects I am the same, could all trace of this product of my most intense deliberations have vanished so completely from my unfathomable mind, that the very title of that little tract, as it lies inscribed in your letter before me, should stare back at me like something cold and alien, indeed that I cannot grasp it at once as a familiar image made up of connected words, but can comprehend it only word by word, as though I were setting eyes on these particular Latin words in this combination for the very first time? But of course I am the same person and these questions are rhetorical – rhetoric which may be good enough for women or the House of Commons, but the powers of which, so greatly overestimated in our time, are insufficient to penetrate to the heart of things. However, I must further explain to you my inner state, a strange unaccountable contrariness, if you like, a disease of the spirit, if you are to understand the unbridgeable gulf that divides me as much from the literary works that I imagine to lie ahead of me as from those already achieved, which now strike me as so alien that I hesitate to acknowledge them as mine.

I do not know which to admire more, your solicitous benevolence or the incredible acuity of your memory, when you recall the various little schemes which occupied me during our agreeable days of inspiration together. I did indeed wish to write about the first years of the reign of our late glorious sovereign Henry the Eighth! The notes my grandfather, the Duke of Exeter, left concerning the negotiations with France and Portugal provided me with some foundations. And then from Sallust during those happy animated days I imbibed, as through free-flowing pipes, an understanding of form, of that deep true inner form which can be apprehended only beyond the domain of rhetorical display, and of which it can no longer be said that it organises content, since it permeates it, elevates it and creates poetry and truth together, a counterpart of eternal forces, a thing as glorious as algebra and music. This was my most dearly cherished plan.

What a thing is man that he should draw up plans!

I toyed with other projects too. Your gracious letter conjures these up before me also. They dance before me, every one of them bloated with a drop of my blood, like sad mosquitoes on a gloomy wall no longer reached by the bright sunshine of those happy days.

I wanted to unlock the myths and fables the Ancients have bequeathed to us, in which painters and sculptors take such endless spontaneous delight, and show them to be hieroglyphs of a secret inexhaustible wisdom whose breath, as from behind a veil, I sometimes thought I felt.

I remember that project. I don't know what spiritual and sensual impulse lay behind it: as the harried stag longs to plunge into the water, so I yearned to assume the radiant naked bodies of those dryads and sirens, of Narcissus and Proteus, Perseus and Actaeon: I wanted to merge with them and speak for them in tongues. That is what I wanted. And there was much besides that I wanted. I thought of assembling a collection of apophthegms like the one Julius Caesar compiled: you recall the reference to it in one of Cicero's letters. In this I intended to set out the most memorable sayings I had managed to collect while associating with the learned men and brilliant women of our time, specially gifted individuals from among the common folk, or cultured and distinguished people met with on my travels; to these I would add fine maxims and reflections from the works of the Ancients and the Italians, and whatever ornaments of thought might come my way in books, manuscripts or conversation; and besides this, accounts of especially impressive processions and festivities, remarkable crimes and cases of insanity, descriptions of the greatest and most characteristic buildings of the Netherlands, France and Italy, and much else. The whole work, however, was to bear the title *Nosce teipsum*.

To sum up: in my state of, as it were, permanent intoxication at that time, all of existence appeared to be one great unity: there seemed no contradiction between the spiritual and corporeal world, any more than between courtly and brutish creatures, art and non-art, solitude and company; I sensed the hand of Nature everywhere, in the divagations of madness as much as in the extreme refinements of Spanish ceremonial; in the clumsinesses of youthful peasants no less than in the sweetest allegories; and in all Nature I was conscious of myself; when in my hunting-lodge I drank foaming lukewarm milk some dishevelled wench had milked into a wooden pail from the swelling udder of a lovely soft-eyed cow, this seemed to me no different from imbibing the sweet and foaming spiritual sustenance of a folio volume as I sat in the window seat of my study. Each was like the other: neither conceded anything to the other as regards either its dreamlike transcendent nature or its powerful physicality, and so things continued at every turn across the whole spectrum of life; everywhere I was involved in things, never conscious of illusion: or rather, I felt everything to be allegory and each creature a key to something else, and I felt sure I was the one capable of seizing each of them one after the other by the root and unlocking the meaning of as many other creatures as each of them would fit. This explains the title I intended to give to my encyclopaedic book.

To someone responsive to these sentiments, it may appear the well-designed plan of a divine Providence that my spirit should sink from such inflated presumption to the extreme state of despondency and impotence that is now its perman-ent condition. But such religious notions have no power over me; they belong to the spiders' webs which my thoughts shoot through, out into the void, while so many of their companions get caught and come to rest there. For me the mysteries of faith have condensed into a sublime allegory, which arches over the meadows of my life like a luminous rainbow, ever at a constant distance, ever ready to recede should it occur to me to hurry over and try to wrap myself in the hem of its raiment.

But, my esteemed friend, mundane concepts too withdraw

from me in the same way. How should I attempt to describe these strange spiritual torments to you, this snatching of fruit-laden branches from my outstretched hands, this retreat of murmuring waters from my thirsting lips?

My condition, in short, is this: I have completely lost the capacity to think or to speak coherently about anything at all.

First, I gradually found it impossible to discuss any higher or more general topic, and thus to use the words everyone is accustomed to using readily and almost without thought. I felt inexplicably uncomfortable merely pronouncing words like 'spirit', 'soul' or 'body'. I found it inwardly impossible to express an opinion about affairs at court, events in parliament, or what you will. And this not out of considerateness of any kind, for as you know I am candid to the point of recklessness; it was rather that the abstract words the tongue must naturally use if any proposition is to see the light of day disintegrated in my mouth like mouldy mushrooms. Once as I was rebuking my four-year-old daughter Katharine Pompilia for some childish lie, and trying to make her realise the necessity of always being truthful, the principles forming on my lips suddenly assumed such crude and garish colours, all running into one another, that I reeled off the rest of my sentence as best I could as if I had been taken ill – and indeed my face was ashen and my temples throbbing violently – then left the child, slamming the door behind me, and only began to recover as I rode my horse at a fair gallop across the lonely meadow.

Gradually, however, this affliction spread like an all-corroding rust. Even in ordinary humdrum conversations, all those pronouncements that are normally made casually and with a sleepwalker's assurance struck me as so questionable that I had to give up taking part in such discussions altogether. I was filled with an inexplicable rage that I had difficulty in concealing whenever I heard things like: such and such a business has turned out well or badly for this person or that; Sheriff N. is a wicked man but T. the preacher is a good man; the tenant farmer M. is to be pitied as his sons are spendthrifts, another fellow to be envied since his daughters are good housekeepers; that family is on the rise, another in decline. All this appeared to me as unfounded, mendacious and unprovable as it could possibly be. My mind compelled me to examine everything that arose in such discussions from uncannily close up: just as I had once looked at a patch of skin on my little finger under a magnifying glass and found it resembled a pitted, furrowed field, I now went about scrutinising people and their actions. I was no longer able to observe them with the simplifying gaze of habit. I broke everything down into its constituent parts, those parts into further parts, and could no longer encompass anything under a single concept. Individual words swam around me: they dissolved into eyes that stared at me and obliged me to stare back: now they have become whirlpools I feel giddy looking down into, which spin round incessantly, and once passed through lead into the void.

I attempted to escape from this predicament into the intellectual world of the Ancients. Plato I avoided; I dreaded the perils of his figurative flights of fancy. I intended to be guided principally by Seneca and Cicero. I hoped to be cured by the harmony of their orderly and finite concepts. But I was unable to cross into their realm. I understood these concepts well enough: I watched the wonderful interplay of ideas rise before me like those splendid waterworks that keep golden balls in play. I was able to hover round them and observe them play with one another; but they were concerned solely with each other, and the deepest, most individual aspects of my thinking were excluded from their roundelay. A terrible sense of loneliness came over me in their company; I felt like someone locked in a garden amongst eyeless statues; I fled back into the open.

Since then I have been leading an existence which I fear you will scarcely be able to comprehend, so insipid and lacking in ideas has it become; an existence, however, which admittedly differs little from my neighbours', my relatives', and that of most of the kingdom's land-owning nobility, and which is not without its happy and invigorating moments. It is not easy for me to convey what these positive moments consist in; once again, words seem to leave me in the lurch. For what is revealed to me at such moments, when some object from my everyday surroundings becomes filled with higher life, like a brimming vessel, is something that has never been named before, indeed, is scarcely nameable. I cannot expect you to understand without giving an illustration, and I beg your indulgence over the banality of my examples. A watering-can, a barrow abandoned in a field, a dog in the sun, a humble churchyard, a cripple, a little farmhouse – any of these might become the receptacle for my revelation. Each of these objects, and a thousand others like them which the indifferent eye normally glosses over as self-evident, can for me, at any moment and without my having the slightest power to induce it, suddenly assume a sublime and deeply moving character which words seem to me utterly inadequate to express. Indeed, it may even be the image of an absent object that is mysteriously selected to be filled to the brim with this gentle, swiftly rising flood of divine feeling. Thus, a short while ago I had given orders for poison to be liberally strewn about for the rats in the milk-cellar on one of my farms. Towards evening I rode off and, as you can imagine, thought no more about the matter. Then, as my horse was plodding across the deeply furrowed land with nothing more alarming in the vicinity than a startled brood of quail taking flight, and the large orb of the sun setting over rolling fields in the distance, suddenly the image of that cellar opened up within me, seething with the death-throes of the colony of rats. It was all there within me: the cool musty air of the cellar filled with the sharp sweet smell of the poison and the piercing death-cries breaking against the mouldering walls; the knotted impotent convulsions and the desperate scurrying to and fro; the frenetic search for a way out; the cold look of fury when two of the creatures would meet at a blocked crevice. But why am I trying to use words again when I have forsworn them! You remember, my friend, the wonderful description in Livy of the last hours before the destruction of Alba Longa? The people roaming through the streets they will never see again . . . taking leave of the very stones on the ground . . . I tell you, my friend,

everything was there within me, and the burning of Carthage
too; but this was more, it was more divine and more bestial;
and it was present, totally, sublimely present to me. There was
a mother whose dying young lay twitching beside her, and as
they expired she did not stare at them, or at the implacable stone
walls, but out into thin air, or through the air into the void, and
as she stared she ground her teeth. If there were ever a slave on
duty standing in impotent horror close to Niobe as she turned to
stone, he must have endured what I endured when within me the
soul of that animal bared its teeth against a monstrous fate.

Forgive me for this account, but do not imagine that what
filled my soul was pity. If you think this, I should have chosen my
example very ineptly. It was much more and much less than pity:
an overwhelming involvement, a flowing into those creatures or a
feeling that the fluid continuum of life and death, of dream and
waking, had momentarily flowed into them – but where from?
For what could it have had to do with pity, or with intelligible
human association of ideas, when on another evening, under a
nut tree, I came across a half-empty watering-can forgotten by
a gardener's boy, and when this watering-can – the water in it
darkened by the shadow of the tree, and a beetle paddling across
the glassy surface from one dark shore to the other – when this
configuration of trivial things thrills me with such a sense of
the presence of infinity, thrills me from the roots of my hair to
the marrow of my heels, that I feel the urge to break out into
words such as I know, if I could find them, would force those
cherubim I don't believe in to descend, so that I immediately
turn from that spot in silence, and weeks later, when I catch
sight of the nut tree, pass it with a shy sidelong glance, because
I do not wish to scare away the residual aura of the miraculous
enveloping its trunk, or to dispel the more than earthly tremors
that still emanate from the bushes near by. In these moments
the lowliest creature, a dog, a rat, a beetle, or a stunted apple
tree, a cart track winding its way over the hill, a moss-covered
stone, means more to me than the most beautiful, most yielding
beloved of my happiest night. These mute creatures and some-

times inanimate objects rise to greet me with such a presence, such a plenitude of love, that my delighted eye fails to alight on any lifeless spot in their vicinity. Everything, whatever exists, whatever I can remember, whatever my confused thoughts touch upon, seems to be its own something. Even my own weight, my normally dull brain, seems to me to be a special something; I feel a delightful, simply inexhaustible interplay inside me and around me, and amid this play of substances there is not one I should not be capable of flowing into. At such times I feel as if my body consisted entirely of ciphers, which reveal everything to me. Or as if we could enter into a new, more aware relationship with the whole of existence, and begin to think with our hearts. But once this strange enchantment recedes, I find I have nothing to say about it; I should be as hard put to find rational words to describe what this harmony interfusing myself and the entire world consisted of, or how it made itself manifest to me, as I should to give a precise account of the movements of my entrails or the surging of my blood.

Apart from these extraordinary occasions, which incidentally I scarcely know whether to attribute to the spirit or to the body, I lead a life of almost unbelievable emptiness, and have difficulty in concealing my inner torpor from my wife, and the indifference I feel toward the affairs of the estate from my retainers. It is I think only the sound, strict upbringing I owe to my late father, and the habit acquired early in life of leaving no hour unoccupied, that enable me to keep an adequate outward grip on my affairs, and to maintain appearances appropriate to my personal dignity and station.

I am having one wing of my house altered, and now and then discuss the progress of the work with the architect; I manage my estate myself and no doubt my tenants and employees find me rather more taciturn, if no less considerate, than I used to be. Not one of them, doffing his cap outside his front door as I ride by of an evening, has any idea that my gaze, which he is wont to meet respectfully, is sweeping in silent longing across the rotten planks under which he digs up worms for bait, and through the

narrow, barred window into the small musty room, where the low
bed in the corner, with its brightly coloured sheets, seems always
to be waiting for someone to be born or die; that my eye lingers
long over the ugly puppies or the cat slinking lithely through
the flower-pots, and that amongst all these crude and wretched
objects of a peasant's life it is searching for the one object whose
unassuming form, whose presence lying or leaning there unno-
ticed, whose mute existence might become the source of that
mysterious wordless infinite delight. For my nameless feeling of
bliss is more likely to arise from a distant lonely shepherd's fire
than a vision of the starry heavens, from the chirping of one last
cricket close to death when the autumn wind has begun to drive
wintry clouds across the desolate fields than from the majestic
booming of the organ. And in my mind I sometimes compare
myself to the orator Crassus, of whom it was reported that he
became so inordinately fond of a tame moray eel, a dull, mute,
red-eyed fish in his ornamental pond, that it became the talk of
the town, and that when on one occasion Domitius reproached
him in the Senate for having shed tears over the death of this
fish, wanting to make him out to be a semi-imbecile, Crassus
roundly replied: 'Then I did at the death of my fish what you did
at the death of neither your first wife nor your second.'

I don't know how often this Crassus with his moray eel has
struck me as a mirror image of myself, projected across the
chasm of the centuries. But not because of the answer he gave
to Domitius. His answer won the scoffers over to his side, so
that the incident concluded as a joke. No, I am affected by the
case itself, the case that would have remained the same even if
Domitius had wept bloody tears of genuine anguish over his
wife. He would still have been confronted by Crassus and his
tears over his moray eel. And something indefinable about this
figure, his absurd and contemptible status in a Senate engaged in
ruling the world and debating lofty issues, takes hold of me and
compels me to think about him in a way that seems completely
foolish the moment I attempt to put it into words.

Occasionally the image of Crassus comes into my mind at

night, lodging there like a splinter around which everything seethes, pulsates and festers. Then I feel as though I were myself in ferment, throwing up bubbles, boiling, coruscating. And the whole thing is a kind of feverish thinking, but thinking in a medium which is more immediate, fluid and aglow than words. Equally it is like so many whirlpools, which do not however, like the whirlpools of language, seem to lead into the abyss, but somehow deep into myself and into the very womb of peace.

My esteemed friend, I have troubled you unduly with this protracted description of my inexplicable condition, which normally remains sealed within me.

You were gracious enough to express your dissatisfaction at no longer receiving any book written by me 'to compensate you for having to forego my company'. At that moment I felt, with a certainty not wholly without pain, that neither in the coming year, nor the year after, nor during the remaining years of my life will I ever write another book either in English or in Latin: and this for a reason the embarrassing strangeness of which I leave it to your infinite intellectual superiority and unclouded eye to classify in the realm of spiritual and bodily phenomena that extends so harmoniously before you: namely, because the language in which it might perhaps be granted me not only to write but to think is neither Latin nor English nor Italian nor Spanish, but a language of which I do not know one word, a language in which mute things speak to me, and in which one day, in my grave, I shall perhaps answer for myself before an unknown judge.

I wish it were vouchsafed me, in the closing words of what is presumably the last letter I shall write to Francis Bacon, to sum up all the love and gratitude, all the boundless admiration for my greatest spiritual benefactor and the foremost Englishman of my times, that I harbour and shall continue to harbour in my heart until it bursts in death.

A. D. 1603, this 22nd day of August
Phi. Chandos

Lucidor

Figures for an Unwritten Comedy

Towards the end of the 1870s Frau von Murska was residing in a small suite at one of the hotels in the Inner City. She went under a minor but not wholly obscure aristocratic name and from what she put about it seemed that a family estate in the Russian part of Poland, which by rights belonged to her and her children, was for the moment being held in trust or withheld from the rightful owners on some other grounds. Her circumstances appeared to be embarrassed, but really only for the moment. Together with her grown-up daughter Arabella, her half-grown-up son Lucidor, and an elderly chambermaid, she occupied three bedrooms and a drawing-room, with windows giving out onto the Kärntnerstrasse. Here she had hung a few family portraits, engravings and miniatures around the walls, covered a pedestal table with a piece of old satin embroidered with a crest and placed a few silver pots and baskets of good eighteenth-century French workmanship upon it, and here she received her guests. She had paid calls and dropped off letters and as she had an incredible number of 'connections' in every sphere, very soon a salon of a kind was established. It was one of those rather indeterminate salons, which were regarded as 'acceptable' or 'unacceptable' depending on the rigour of the person passing judgement. In any case, Frau von Murska was anything but vulgar or a bore, and her daughter was even more remarkably distinguished in character and bearing and quite extraordinarily beautiful. Anyone calling between four and six was certain to find the mother at home and almost never without company; the daughter was not always to be seen, and only family intimates were acquainted with the thirteen- or fourteen-year-old Lucidor.

Frau von Murska was a woman of real culture, with nothing of the commonplace about her. In Viennese high society, to which she vaguely thought of herself as belonging, without however coming into more than very peripheral contact with it, she would have been given a hard time as a 'blue-stocking'. But in her head there reigned such a confused medley of adventures, intuitions, hypotheses, errors, enthusiasms, experiences and apprehensions, that it was simply not worth pondering what she might have acquired from books. Her conversation galloped from one subject to the next, discovering the most improbable connections; her restlessness could arouse pity – hearing her talk one knew, without her needing to mention it, that she suffered from insomnia to the point of madness and consumed herself with worries, conjectures and misplaced hopes – but listening to her was very remarkable and entertaining nonetheless, and without intending to be indiscreet, she occasionally contrived to be so in the most appalling manner. In short, she was a fool, but of the most agreeable kind. She was a kind-hearted, basically charming, and not in the least bit ordinary woman. But a difficult life, which she had not been equal to, had left her in such a state of bewilderment that now in her forty-second year she was a fantastical creature. Most of her ideas and judgements were original and of great spiritual refinement, but they were almost always wide of the mark and wholly inappropriate to the specific persons or circumstances in question. The closer a person was to her, the less clearly was she able to view him or her; and it would have been a breach of divine order had she not harboured the most wrong-headed notions about her two children and blindly acted in accordance with them. Arabella in her eyes was an angel, Lucidor a hard and rather heartless little creature. Arabella was a thousand times too good for this world, while Lucidor was admirably cut out for it. Arabella was actually the spitting image of her deceased father – a proud, dissatisfied, impatient, very handsome man, quick to scorn but concealing it beneath excellent good form, respected or envied by other men and loved by many women, and of a distinctly dry temperament. Little Lucidor by contrast was all heart. But perhaps I should say at once at this point that Lucidor was not a young gentleman at all but a girl, and called Lucile. Like all Frau von Murska's notions, that of having her younger daughter appear *en travesti* for the duration of their stay in Vienna had occurred to her in a flash, and yet had the most complicated origins and ramifications. What was principally involved was the idea of making an adroit move against an elderly, mysterious but fortunately actually existing uncle living in Vienna, on whose account perhaps – all these hopes and conjectures were extremely vague – she had originally chosen this city in particular to reside in. At the same time the disguise also had other, very real, very immediate advantages. Living with *one* daughter was easier than with two not quite of the same age – the girls were almost four years apart – since one could get away with fewer expenses. And then it was an even better, more appropriate position for Arabella to be the only daughter rather than the elder one; and the winsome young 'brother', as a sort of groom, made the fair creature's beauty stand out in relief.

Several chance circumstances stood them in good stead. Frau von Murska's notions were never wholly based on unreality, it was just that she linked the actual or given with what seemed possible or attainable to her imagination in rather eccentric ways. Five years earlier Lucile's beautiful hair – as a child of eleven at the time, she had survived a bout of typhus – had had to be cut short. Furthermore, Lucile had a preference for riding astride; it was a habit going back to the time when she and the Little Russian peasant lads would ride the horses on the family estate to water bareback. Lucile accepted the disguise as she accepted many other things. She was of a patient disposition, and even the greatest absurdity very easily becomes a habit. Moreover, since she was painfully shy, she was delighted with the thought of never having to appear in the drawing-room and play the grown-up young lady. The old chambermaid was the only one in the secret; strangers didn't notice anything at all. To be the first to detect something peculiar is never easy; for in general it is not given to human beings to see the true state of things. Besides, Lucile really did have boyishly narrow hips and no other feature that might have betrayed the girl in her too much. And indeed the matter remained undisclosed and unsuspected, and when events took a turn that was to make a bride or something still more feminine of little Lucidor, all the world was very much surprised.

Naturally so beautiful and in every sense attractive-looking a young person as Arabella did not remain long without several more or less declared admirers. Amongst these, Vladimir was by far the most significant. He was remarkably good-looking and had especially fine hands. He was more than well to do and completely independent; his parents had died and he had no siblings. His father had been an Austrian officer of the bourgeoisie, his mother a countess from a very well known Baltic family. Among all those who paid Arabella their attentions, he was the only genuinely suitable match. Added to all this was a very special circumstance which quite enchanted Frau von Murska. It just so happened that he had some family connection with the difficult, reclusive and all-important uncle, the same person on whose account they were living in Vienna, and on whose account Lucile had become Lucidor. This uncle, who occupied an entire floor of the Buquoy Palace in the Wallnerstrasse and had once been a gentleman much talked about, had responded to Frau von Murska unpropitiously. Although she really was the widow of his nephew (or more precisely, his father's brother's grandson), she had only managed to see him the third time she called, and after that she had never once been invited for so much as breakfast or a cup of tea. On the other hand, he had with rather an ill grace consented that Lucidor should be sent to see him some time. It was one of the eccentricities of this interesting old gentleman that he could not stand women, whether old or young. There was the faint hope, however, that he might one day take a bountiful interest in a young gentleman who, even if he did not bear the same name, was nonetheless his blood relation. And in a highly precarious situation, even so tenuous a hope was infinitely precious. Lucidor had in fact ridden over alone once on the mother's orders but not been received, and had been very happy about that, though Frau von Murska was incensed, especially since nothing further ensued and the precious thread seemed to have snapped. So now Vladimir was the truly providential man sent to retie it through this double association. To set things properly in motion Lucidor would sometimes be called in discreetly when Vladimir was visiting mother and daughter, and fate very obligingly decreed that Vladimir should take a liking to the lad. At the very first meeting he asked whether Lucidor would from time to time go riding with him, which, after a rapid exchange of glances between Arabella and her mother, was gratefully assented to. Vladimir's fondness for the younger brother of a girl whom he was very much in love with was only natural; there is scarcely anything more agreeable than a look of undisguised admiration in the eyes of a fine fourteen-year-old boy.

Increasingly, Frau von Murska went down on her knees to Vladimir. This, like most of her mother's affectations, irritated Arabella, and although she enjoyed seeing Vladimir, almost despite herself she began to flirt with one of his rivals, Herr von Imfanger, an affable and very elegant Tyrolean, half-gentleman, half-farmer, even though he did not come into question as a suitable match. When on one occasion her mother cautiously ventured to reproach Arabella for not treating Vladimir as he had a right to expect, Arabella gave a dismissive reply in which more coldness and contempt for Vladimir was concentrated than she really felt. Lucidor-Lucile happened to be present. The blood rushed to her heart and as abruptly left it. A sharp pang shot through her: she felt fear, pain and anger all at once. She was quite dumbfounded by her sister. Arabella had always been a stranger to her. At this moment she seemed quite horrifying, and

she could not have said whether she hated or admired her. Then
everything dissolved in boundless misery. She ran and locked
herself in her room. If someone had told her that she was in
love with Vladimir, she perhaps would not have understood. She
behaved as she was bound to, automatically, shedding tears whose
true meaning she did not understand. She sat down and wrote an
ardent love letter to Vladimir. Not on her own behalf, however,
but for Arabella. It had often vexed her that her handwriting was
so like Arabella's as to be readily mistaken for it. She had forced
herself to adopt a different, rather ugly script. But she could
make use of the earlier one, which was actually well suited to her
hand, at any time. Indeed, basically she found it easier to write
like that. The letter was of the kind that only those who have
stopped thinking and are actually beside themselves can write.
It belied Arabella's entire nature: but then of course that was
what it aimed to do, what it had to do. It was highly improbable
as an expression of violent inner upheaval, but then for that very
reason in certain respects quite probable. If Arabella had been
capable of loving deeply and devotedly and in a sudden flash of
illumination become aware of this, she might conceivably have
expressed herself in this way and been capable of this degree of
boldness and passionate contempt for herself, for the Arabella
everybody knew. The letter was certainly unusual, but still even
to a cool indifferent reader not utterly implausible as a letter from
a secretly passionate, unpredictable young lady. To a man in love
moreover, the woman he loves is always an incalculable creature.
And then finally it was the kind of letter a man in his situation
always desires and considers it possible he might receive. Let
me say here that the letter did indeed reach Vladimir's hands
– on the stairs the very next afternoon, with Lucidor following
him softly, cautiously calling out and whispering to him as his
beautiful sister's supposed awkward, agitated go-between. Of
course a postscript had been urgently added requesting, indeed
imploring him not to be angry if to begin with not the slightest
change in Arabella's behaviour towards either her beloved or
anybody else should be discernible. He was adjured too not to

let on by so much as a word or a look that he knew himself to be tenderly loved.

A few days went by in which Vladimir encountered Arabella only briefly, and never alone. He met her as she requested; she met him as she had stipulated in advance. He felt both happy and unhappy. Only now did he realise how fond of her he was. The situation was calculated to make him boundlessly impatient. Lucidor, with whom he now rode daily and in whose company he felt at ease as in almost no one else's, observed the changes in his friend, his growing uncontrollable impatience, with horror and delight. Another letter followed, almost more tender than the first, another moving request not to disturb their much threatened happiness in their present precarious situation, to be content with these declarations and at most respond to them, with Lucidor as intermediary, in writing. Every second or third day now a letter was sent and received. Vladimir's days passed happily and so did Lucidor's. The tone they adopted when they were together had changed, and they now had an inexhaustible topic of conversation. Whenever they dismounted in some coppice in the Prater and Lucidor handed Vladimir his latest letter, he watched his features with apprehensive pleasure as he read. Sometimes he asked questions that were almost indiscreet; but Vladimir was amused by the excitement and intelligence of this boy entangled in their love affair, by something about him that made him appear more gentle and attractive by the day; and he had to admit that though normally reserved and proud, he would find it hard not to be able to talk to Lucidor about Arabella. Lucidor sometimes also adopted the pose of a misogynist, of a knowing and in a childish way cynical young fellow. His observations were far from banal; moreover, he had a way of lacing them with what medics term 'introspective truths'. But Vladimir, who was not short of self-esteem, made a point of informing him that the love he inspired, and inspired in such a creature as Arabella, was of a very special and quite incomparable kind. At such moments Lucidor found Vladimir all the more admirable and himself pitiful and small. They got around to discussing marriage, and for Lucidor this topic was a torment, for then Vladimir was concerned almost exclusively with the Arabella of real life instead of the Arabella of the letters. Lucidor was also mortally afraid of any decision, any precipitous change. All he could think about was how to prolong the situation as it was. There was no saying what it cost the poor creature to maintain a provisional equilibrium in so outwardly and inwardly precarious a situation for days, for weeks – further than that he hadn't the strength to contemplate. But since the mission that had fallen to his lot was to arrange something with the uncle for the family, he continued to do his level best. Vladimir began to go with him; it evidently amused the eccentric old gentleman not to stand on ceremony with younger people, and for Lucidor an hour's conversation with him was a truly painful ordeal. And yet nothing seemed further from the old man's mind than the idea of doing something for his relatives. Lucidor was unable to lie yet wanted to placate his mother in all things. As for the mother, the lower the hopes she had placed in the uncle sank, the greater grew her impatience at observing that things between Vladimir and Arabella did not seem to be approaching a decision. The wretched people she was dependent on in money matters were beginning to write off each of these glittering prospects. Her anxiety and laboriously concealed impatience were communicated to everyone, especially to the unfortunate Lucidor, in whose head conflicting and intolerable thoughts were swirling. But in the strange school of life to which he was now committed, he was to receive a few sharper and more subtle lessons still.

Not a word was ever said explicitly about Arabella's double nature. But somehow the notion surfaced of its own accord: the daytime Arabella was diffident, coquettish, punctilious, self-confident, worldly and dry almost to excess, the night-time Arabella, who wrote to her lover by candle-light, was yielding and ardent almost beyond measure. Coincidentally or by some decree of fate, this corresponded to a secret split in Vladimir's nature too. Like every animate being, he also, broadly speaking, had his day and night sides. His rather dry hauteur and lofty and steadfast ambition with no trace of vulgar striving stood opposed to quite other impulses, or not stood exactly, since they ducked and tried to hide among the shadows, ever ready to plunge below the twilight threshold into scarcely conscious realms. In the past a fantastical sensuality which enabled him to dream of entering the being even of an animal, a dog say or a swan, had taken almost complete possession of his soul. He did not like to recall this period of transition from boyhood into youth. But something of it was still there inside him, and now this night side of his being, never visited by his thoughts, wilfully deserted, was being scanned by a dark mysterious light: his love for the other, invisible Arabella. Had the daytime Arabella happened to be his wife or become his mistress, he would always have remained on matter-of-fact terms with her and never conceded the phantoms of a wilfully repressed childhood a place in his life. He thought of the one dwelling in darkness in a different way and wrote to her also in a different way. What should Lucidor do when his friend asked to be granted something more, some livelier token than these lines on bare white paper? Lucidor was alone with his anxieties, his confusion, his love. The daytime Arabella was of no help to him. Indeed it was as though, driven by some demon, she were actually playing against him. The colder, more erratic, worldly and coquettish she was, the more Vladimir hoped for and demanded of her sister. He pleaded so successfully that Lucidor could not find the courage to refuse. And even had he done so, his delicate pen would have been at a loss for words to express such a refusal. One night Vladimir was allowed to believe he had been received, and unreservedly received, by Arabella in Lucidor's own room. Somehow Lucidor had managed to darken the window overlooking the Kärntnerstrasse so completely that one couldn't see further than one's nose. Clearly their voices had to be reduced to a barely audible whisper: only a door separated them from the old chambermaid. Where Lucidor spent the night remained undisclosed: but evidently he was not in the secret and some excuse was found for him. The strange thing was that Arabella wore her beautiful hair tightly bound in a thick scarf, and gently but firmly refused to allow her lover to undo it. But this was almost the only thing that she refused. Several nights elapsed bearing no resemblance to this one, but then another followed which did resemble it, and again Vladimir was supremely happy. Perhaps these were the happiest days of his entire life. When he was with Arabella during the day, the security of his nocturnal happiness gave his voice a special tone. He began to find a peculiar pleasure in the fact that she was so unaccountably different by day: her command over herself, never allowing her to forget herself by so much as a look or gesture, was in its way enchanting. He thought he noticed that week by week she was becoming colder and colder towards him the more tenderly she had received him during the night. At all events, he did not wish to appear less artful, less controlled himself. Since he was complying so unconditionally with this mysteriously powerful female will, he believed that to some extent he was earning his nocturnal happiness. He was beginning to derive the greatest enjoyment precisely from her double nature. That the woman who appeared not to belong to him at all should nonetheless belong to him, and that the same woman who was capable of giving herself so unreservedly should also know how to assert herself as such an untouched, untouchable presence, was all dizzying to experience, like repeatedly quaffing from a magic cup. He recognised that he ought to thank fate on his knees for having granted him a delight so uniquely attuned to the secret desires of his nature. He poured all this out in torrents both to himself and to Lucidor. Nothing could have aroused more mortal terror in poor Lucidor.

Meanwhile Arabella, the real one, had turned so decisively away from Vladimir during these same weeks that he must at any time surely have noticed, were he not under the strangest compulsion to interpret everything mistakenly. Without his actually giving himself away, she sensed a certain something between them that hadn't been there before. They had always understood each other, they still understood each other; their day sides were mutually compatible; they could have a successful rational marriage. She and Herr von Imfanger did not understand each other, but he appealed to her. She now felt more strongly that Vladimir did not appeal to her in this way; the unaccountable something that seemed to vibrate from him to her made her impatient. It wasn't courtship, neither was it flattery; she couldn't get clear quite what it was, but she didn't appreciate it. Imfanger must surely know she liked him. Vladimir for his part still believed he had quite other proof of her regard. The strangest situation thus arose between the two gentlemen. Each believed the other ought to have every reason to be put out or simply to abandon the field. Each found the other's attitude, his untroubled mood, at bottom simply ridiculous. Neither knew what to make of the other, and each regarded the other as a downright fool and coxcomb.

The mother was in the most painful of predicaments. Her various expedients were failing. People she had befriended were leaving her in the lurch. A loan offered under the guise of friendship had been inconsiderately recalled. Vehement decisions always appealed to Frau von Murska. She resolved to break up the household in Vienna overnight, take leave of her acquaintances by letter, and seek refuge somewhere, if need be on the sequestered estate in the steward's family home. Arabella was not pleased to hear of this decision, but despair was alien to her nature. Lucidor had to lock her genuine and measureless despair away within herself. Several nights had elapsed since she had called her lover to her. She wanted to summon him again tonight. The evening discussion between Arabella and her mother, the decision to depart, the impossibility of preventing the departure – all this had hit her like a hammer-blow. Whenever she thought she might resort to desperate measures, put everything behind her, confess all to her mother, above all reveal to her lover who the Arabella of his nights had been, an icy fear of his disappointment and anger passed through her. She felt like a criminal, but only towards him, she didn't think about the others. She couldn't see him tonight. She felt she would die of shame, of fear and confusion. Instead of holding him in her arms, she wrote to him one last time. It was the humblest, most moving letter, and nothing was less suited to it than the name Arabella with which she signed it. She had never really hoped to become his wife. A few short years, even one year living with him as his mistress would be immeasurable happiness. But even that could and must not be. He must not ask, must not press her, she implored him. He should come and visit her again tomorrow, but only towards evening. The day after tomorrow – they might already have left. Later some day he might discover, understand, she wanted to add 'forgive', but the word seemed inconceivable in Arabella's mouth, and so she didn't write it down. She hardly slept a wink, got up early, sent the letter off to Vladimir via the hotel porter. The morning was taken up with packing. After lunch, without mentioning anything, she drove out to the uncle. The idea had come to her during the night. She would find the right words and arguments to soften the strange man. The miracle would happen and that firmly tied purse of his open up. She was not thinking about the reality of all these things, only about her mother, about the situation, about her love. She would fall at her mother's feet with the money or the letter in her hand and beg her – for what? her overwrought, tormented brain was almost giving out – of course! Why obviously, that they stay on in Vienna, that everything remain the same. She found the uncle at home. The details of this scene and the peculiar course it took cannot be recounted here. Suffice to say she did succeed in softening him – he was on the point of taking the decisive action, but then an old man's whim overturned the decision once again, he would do something for them later, when he couldn't say for certain, so there was an end of it. She drove home, crept up the stairs, and once in her room, squatting on the floor among the suitcases and boxes, she abandoned herself completely to despair. Then she thought she heard Vladimir's voice in the adjoining drawing-room. She tiptoed across to the wall and listened. It was indeed Vladimir – with Arabella, and they were engaged in the strangest altercation with raised voices.

That morning Vladimir had received Arabella's mysterious farewell letter. Nothing had ever smitten his heart like this before. He felt there was something dark between them, but not between their hearts. He felt he had enough love and strength within him to learn, to understand, and to forgive – whatever it might turn out to be. He had grown too fond of the incomparable beloved of his nights to live without her. Curiously, he was not thinking of the real Arabella at all, and he found it quite strange that she should be the one he must approach in order to placate and console her, and win her wholly and forever. He arrived to find the mother in the drawing-room alone. She was as agitated, confused and fantastical as ever. He was more changed than she had ever seen him. He kissed her hands, spoke out, saying everything in an emotional awkward manner. He begged her to permit him an interview alone with Arabella. Frau von Murska was delighted and with no transition became perfectly ecstatic. The improbable was her element. She hastened to fetch Arabella, urging her not to refuse the noble young man her consent now that things had turned out so splendidly. Arabella was completely astounded. 'This is not the way things are between us,' she said coolly. 'One never knows where one is with men,' her mother replied and sent her into the drawing-room. Vladimir was embarrassed, red-faced and emotional. Arabella was more and more convinced that Herr von Imfangen was right to consider Vladimir a very peculiar gentleman indeed. Put out by her coolness, Vladimir begged her to drop her mask at last. Arabella had absolutely no idea what mask it was she was supposed to drop. Vladimir had become tender and angry simultaneously, a mixture so little to Arabella's liking that eventually she ran out of the room and left him standing there. Vladimir in his infinite bewilderment was closer to regarding her as mad for her intimation that she regarded him as such, and that a third party was of her opinion on the matter. At this point Vladimir would have launched into a hapless monologue if the other door hadn't opened and the strangest figure rushed towards him, embraced him, and slipped to the floor before him. It was Lucidor, but then again not Lucidor but Lucile, an adorable young woman bathed in tears, wearing one of Arabella's morning dresses, her boyishly short hair hidden beneath a tightly bound silk scarf. It was his friend and companion, his mysterious mistress, his beloved, his wife. A dialogue such as the one that now took place life may give birth to and comedy attempt to imitate – but never a short tale.

Whether Lucidor afterwards really did become Vladimir's wife or in some other land continued to be by day what she had already been to him by night, his blissful beloved, can also not be recorded here.

It might be doubted whether Vladimir was a sufficiently worthy person to merit such affectionate devotion. But at all events the full beauty of an unconditionally devoted soul such as Lucile's could not have been revealed under any less unusual circumstances.

Notes

A Chance Glimpse of Happiness

Page 44: *Prater*. Vienna's most fashionable riding and recreational park.

Page 46: *La Fortune*. Hofmannsthal may well have intended to invoke the iconographic tradition depicting Dame Fortune in command of a rudderless boat, which, like the image of her blindfold and turning her wheel, originated in Boethius' late Roman *Consolation of Philosophy*.

The Tale of the 672nd Night

Page 50: *mulberry-coloured complexion*. In a short manuscript summary of this tale dated 19 April 1895, Hofmannsthal writes: 'the servant a 48-year-old, with mulberry-coloured face like the dictator Sulla', as described in Plutarch.

Pages 50–51: *some very great king from the past*. From a note Hofmannsthal made on the back of a second, full manuscript version of the tale, it has been inferred that the king referred to is Alexander the Great, about whom he was also planning a play at the time.

A Cavalry Tale

Page 64: *1848* was a year of revolutions against autocratic governments across Europe, and Italy saw insurrections in Milan and Venice against Austria, and outside Habsburg territory in Rome, Naples and Sicily. In five days of street fighting (18–22 March) the Milanese led by Luciano Manara expelled the Austrian garrison, while in Venice Daniele Manin and his followers entered the arsenal and declared a republic. Responding to Milan's pleas, Charles Albert, King of Sardinia and Piedmont, declared war on Austria in Lombardy, forcing Field Marshal

Radetzky to withdraw to Verona. The liberal Pope Pius IX also sent troops initially but then withdrew, deciding that he could not support a war against Catholic Austria. The Italians were eventually routed at Custoza at the end of July 1848 and Milan was taken shortly after, half the population taking flight. Charles Albert was finally defeated at Novara on 23 March the following year and a disease- and famine-stricken Venice bombarded into submission.

Wallmoden Cuirassiers. The Sixth Dragoons with which Hofmannsthal served in 1894–95 was a distinguished and exclusive cavalry regiment dating back to the Thirty Years' War, and until 1867 was known as the Mährisches Kürassier-Regiment Graf Wallmoden. Sixty per cent of its officers were from the nobility – in letters home Hofmannsthal commented jocularly on the august company he was keeping – and high standards of riding and swordsmanship were maintained. The squadron of the Sixth that served in Italy in 1848 was known as the *Wallmoden-Kürassiere.* Cuirassiers were heavy as against light cavalry (terms relating to both their armaments and horses) and used for frontal attack rather than skirmishing.

Bergamasque costume. Historically the Lombard town of Bergamo, forty kilometres north-east of Milan, had been under both Milanese and Venetian control. Its musical culture, associated with Donizetti and Monteverdi, is celebrated by Debussy in his *Suite Bergamasque.*

Page 65: *seventy-eight cavalrymen.* Hofmannsthal is deliberately specific in giving numbers of casualties and those detailed to guard captured prisoners, guns and cattle (armies were still expected to sustain themselves by foraging), in order to make clear that at the end the squadron is under-strength and Captain Rofrano's disciplinary action necessary. (Carl V. Hansen, 'The Death of First Sergeant Lerch in Hofmannsthal's *Reitergeschichte*: A Military Analysis', *Modern Austrian Literature* 13 (1980), pages 17–26.)

Marshal de Bassompierre's Adventure

Page 75: *Marshal de Bassompierre.* François de Bassompierre (1579–1643), created Marshal of France for services during the Huguenot uprising of 1621, was a leading figure of the era of Louis XIII. His career as a soldier and diplomat came to an end in 1631 when, suspected of plotting against Cardinal Richelieu, he was imprisoned in the Bastille, being released only after Richelieu's death in 1643. While in prison he wrote his memoirs, published in Cologne in 1665, from which Goethe translated two anecdotes, including them in his ground-breaking novella cycle *Entertainments of German Refugees (Unterhaltungen deutscher Ausgewanderten*, 1795), one of which provides the basis for Hofmannsthal's tale.

'Marshal de Bassompierre's Adventure'. After the appearance of the first half of this story on 24 November 1900 in the Vienna newspaper *Die Zeit*, Hofmannsthal was accused of plagiarism in the *Deutsches Volksblatt*. Karl Kraus defended him in the November issue of his *Die Fakel*, declaring that 'what uneducated people are pleased to call plagiarism is in fact citation.' In publishing the second part of his story in *Die Zeit* a week later, Hofmannsthal observed that he had assumed explicit acknowledgement to be unnecessary, since an educated public would have had Goethe's collected works to hand on their shelves.

the Petit Pont. Connecting the Rue Saint Jacques in the Latin Quarter on the South Bank to the Isle de la Cité, where from the Middle Ages the area round Notre Dame had a seedy reputation, as Hofmannsthal would have known from Victor Hugo's novels.

Page 84: *Lorraine*. Where the historical de Bassompierre had his château.

Letter from Lord Chandos

Page 86: *Sallust*. The historiography of Gaius Sallustius Crispus (86–35 BC), notably *The Conspiracy of Catiline* and *The War Against Jugurtha*, is characterised by Thucydidean terseness and imaginative recreation of characters, who are given words such as they might have spoken.

Page 87: *algebra and music*. Hofmannsthal encountered speculative reflections on the analogies between mathematics, music and poetry in the writings of one of his favourite Romantic poets, the mystical Friedrich von Herdenberg (1772–1801) who wrote under the pen-name Novalis.

apophthegms. Introducing his own *Apophthegms New and Old* (1625), Bacon commented that 'Julius Caesar did write a collection of apoph-thegms, as appears in an epistle of Cicero. It is a pitie his booke is lost.'

Nosce teipsum. 'Know thyself.'

Page 91: *Alba Longa*. Fabled to have been founded by Aeneas' son Ascanius in c. 1152 BC and to have been destroyed by Tullus Hostilius some four centuries later with the founding of Rome by Romulus and Remus. The razing of *Carthage* by Scipio Africanus Minor took place at the end of the Third Punic War in 146 BC.

Page 92: *Niobe*. In Ovid's account in Book VI of the *Metamorphoses*, Niobe, wife of Amphion, king of Thebes, refuses to sacrifice to the goddess Latona, who punishes her by sending Apollo and Diana to kill her seven sons and seven daughters. She is turned into a block of marble which continues to shed tears. In art, the classical Niobe group in the Uffizi Gallery ranks with that of the Laocoön, and painters who were inspired by the theme include Tintoretto, Bloemaert, LeBrun, Fragonard and David.

Lucidor

Page 96: *The Russian part of Poland*. The third partition of Poland between Prussia, Austria and Russia along geographical lines in 1795 was essentially ratified at the Congress of Vienna in 1815. The area centred on the Duchy of Warsaw, which Napoleon had created in 1807 as the nucleus of a new Polish national state, retained some autonomy, but former Polish territories in Lithuania, Belorussia and the Ukraine were incorporated into the Russian Empire, and their Catholic inhabitants obliged to convert to Russian Orthodoxy. Poznan in the west was systematically colonised by Lutheran Prussia. Austria's Polish acquisitions to the south, re-christened Galicia, did not suffer religious persecution and throughout the nineteenth century Cracow was an oasis of liberal Polish culture.

Kärntnerstrasse. Running from the Opera off the Ringstrasse – built over the glacis surrounding the medieval Inner City during Franz Joseph's reign – down to St Stephen's Cathedral at its heart, the Kärntnerstrasse boasted some of Vienna's most fashionable shops and coffee-houses and (from 1907) the famous basement cabaret 'Die Fledermaus'.

Page 99: *an Austrian officer of the bourgeoisie*. The point here is that the father had not, like so many of the officers in the Habsburg army, been of the aristocracy. See the second note to page 64.

Buquoy Palace. Originally from Artois, General Karel Bonaventura Buquoy was ennobled by Emperor Ferdinand II von Habsburg for his leadership in the Battle of the White Mountain near Prague in 1620, which effectively ended religious freedom in Bohemia early in the Thirty Years' War. His Czech estates remained in the family until 1945; the Buquoy Palace in Prague is now the French embassy, that in Vienna under lease to the university.

Page 102: *A few days went by*. The dramatic present which runs from this paragraph almost to the end of the story has been rendered in this translation as past, since in English the dramatic present usually has the opposite effect to that intended.

Details of First Publication

The tales included in this selection were first published as follows:

Justice (*Gerechtigkeit*), dated 26 May 1893, first published posthumously in *Loris: Die Prosa des jungen Hofmannsthal*, edited by Max Mell (Berlin: S. Fischer Verlag, 1930).

A Chance Glimpse of Happiness (*Das Glück am Weg*), Vienna: *Deutsche Zeitung,* 30 June 1893; included in Hugo von Hofmannsthal, *Früheste Prosastücke* (Leipzig: Gesellschaft der Freunde der Deutschen Bücherei, 1926).

The Tale of the 672nd Night (*Das Märchen der 672. Nacht*), Vienna: *Die Zeit*, 2 and 16 November 1895; included in Hofmannsthal, *Das Märchen der 672. Nacht und andere Erzählungen* (Vienna: Wiener Verlag, 1905).

A Cavalry Tale (*Reitergeschichte*), Vienna: *Neue Freie Presse*, 25 December 1899; included in *Das Märchen der 672. Nacht.*

Marshal de Bassompierrre's Adventure (*Das Erlebnis des Marschalls von Bassompierre*), Vienna: *Die Zeit*, 24 November and 1 December 1900; included in *Das Märchen der 672. Nacht.*

Letter from Lord Chandos (*Ein Brief*), Berlin: *Der Tag*, 18 and 19 October 1902; included (with title *Brief des Lord Chandos*) in *Das Märchen der 672. Nacht.*

Lucidor, Vienna: *Neue Freie Presse*, 27 March 1910; included in Hofmannsthal, *Gesammelte Werke*, II (Berlin: S. Fischer Verlag, 1924).

Further Reading

Virginia M. Allen, *The Femme Fatale: Erotic Icon* (New York: Whitson, 1983)

Hermann Broch, *Hugo von Hofmannsthal and his Time: The European Imagination 1860–1920* [1975], edited and translated by Michael P. Steinberg (Chicago: Chicago University Press, 1984)

A Companion to the Works of Hugo von Hofmannsthal, edited by Thomas A. Kovach (New York: Camden House, 2002)

Peter Gay, *Schnitzler's Century: The Making of Middle-class Culture 1815–1914* (New York: W. W. Norton, 2002)

The Habsburg Legacy: National Identity in Historical Perspective, edited by Carl E. Schorske and Edward Timms (Edinburgh: Edinburgh University Press, 1994)

Hugo von Hofmannsthal, *Poems and Verse Plays,* bilingual edition edited and translated by Michael Hamburger (New York: Pantheon, 1961)

—— , *Selected Plays & Libretti*, edited and translated by Michael Hamburger et al. (London: Routledge, 1963)

—— , *Selected Prose*, introduction by Hermann Broch, translated by Mary Hottinger et al. (London: Routledge, 1952)

Hofmannsthal: Studies in Commemoration, edited by F. Norman (London: University of London Institute of Germanic Studies, 1963)

Allan Janik and Stephen Toulmin, *Wittgenstein's Vienna* (New York: Simon & Schuster; London: Weidenfeld & Nicolson, 1973)

Jacques Le Rider, *Modernity and Crisis of Identity: Culture and Society in fin-de-siècle Vienna* [1990], translated by Rosemary Morris (Cambridge: Polity Press, 1993)

Kevin McAleer, *Dueling: The Cult of Honor in Fin-de-siècle Germany* (Princeton: Princeton University Press, 1994)

Robert Musil, *The Man without Qualities* (1930–43), translated by Sophie Wilkins and Burton Pike (London: Picador, 1995)

Ritchie Robertson, *The 'Jewish Question' in German Literature 1749–1939: Emancipation and its Discontents* (Oxford: Oxford University Press, 1999)

Joseph Roth, *The Radetzky March* [1932], translated by Joachim Neugroschel (London: Penguin, 1995)

Arthur Schnitzler, *Selected Short Fiction*, translated by J. M. Q. Davies (London: Angel Books, 1999)

Carl E. Schorske, *Fin-de-siècle Vienna: Politics and Culture* (New York: Random House, 1961)

The Vienna Coffeehouse Wits 1890–1938, edited and translated by Harold B. Segel (W. Lafayette: Purdue University Press, 1993)

Robert Vilain, *The Poetry of Hugo von Hofmannsthal and French Symbolism* (Oxford: Oxford University Press, 2000)

Philip Ward, *Hofmannsthal and Greek Myth: Expression and Performance* (Bern: Peter Lang, 2002)

W. E. Yates, *Schnitzler, Hofmannsthal, and the Austrian Theatre* (New Haven: Yale University Press, 1992)

Stefan Zweig, *The World of Yesterday* [introduction by Harry Zohn, 1943] (Lincoln: University of Nebraska Press, 1964)

ANGEL BOOKS

Angel Books publishes new translations of classic foreign literature of the nineteenth and twentieth centuries, in quality paperback editions (occasionally in hardback) with introductions and end-notes, focusing on authors and works not currently or not adequately available in English.

For further information please write to Angel Books,
3 Kelross Road, London N5 2QS
woodangel@ukonline.co.uk

German Fiction

The first English translation of the second of Fontane's series of Berlin novels. At a fashionable spa an affair develops between an itinerant engineer and the delicate, mysterious wife of an army officer – to explode in Germany's bustling new capital. '*Cécile* is written with wit and a controlled fury, and Radcliffe's elegant translation does it superb justice.' – Michael Ratcliffe, *The Observer*

A balanced selection of thirteen of Schnitzler's stories exploring turbulent Viennese inner lives, ranging from the celebrated *Lieutenant Gustl* and *Fräulein Else* to other vintage but lesser-known tales, some of which are translated for the first time. '… masterly psychological observation.' – Charles Osborne, *Sunday Telegraph*

Kleist's *Earthquake in Chile* and *The Betrothal on Santo Domingo*; Tieck's *Eckbert the Fair* and *The Runenberg*; Hoffmann's *Don Giovanni* and *The Jesuit Chapel in G*. 'All the varieties of the German Romantic movement are here – magical, political and aesthetic, and in excellent translations.' – Stephen Plaice, *Times Literary Supplement*

The most substantial selection of Stifter's narratives of the diseased subconscious to appear in English. 'Stifter's stories, richly symbolic and brushed with mystery, are presented in wonderful new translations.' – *Publishers Weekly*

Russian and East European Fiction

Andrey Bely
The Silver Dove
Translated by John Elsworth
978-0-946162-64-2

This first modern Russian novel (1909), by the author of *Petersburg*, whom Nabokov ranked with Proust, Kafka and Joyce, depicts a culture on the brink, in the aftermath of the 1905 revolution. 'Bely depicts a world which is fascinating, full of strange imagery and tormented by passions.' – Isobel Montgomery, *The Guardian*

Vsevolod Garshin
From the Reminiscences of Private Ivanov *and other stories*
Translated by Peter Henry and others
978-0-946162-09-3

Russia's outstanding new writer between Dostoyevsky and the mature Chekhov, Garshin, 'a Hamlet of his time', gave voice to the disturbed conscience of an era that knew the horrors of modern war, the squalors of rapid urbanisation, and a highly explosive political situation. This selection contains almost all his short fiction, including his best-known stories 'The Red Flower', 'The Signal' and *'Attalea Princeps'*. 'A powerful, innovative writer, ably translated.' – *New York Times Book Review*

Jaroslav Hašek
(author of *The Good Soldier Švejk*)
The Bachura Scandal *and other stories and sketches*
Translated by Alan Menhennet
978-0-946162-41-3

These 32 stories of Prague life, most of them translated into English for the first time, revel in the twisted logic of politics and bureaucracy in the Czech capital which was also an Austrian provincial city. 'Animated translations ... Hašek emerges as a prankster who carries his "what if" musings to absurdist heights.' – *The New York Times*

Poetry

GENNADY AYGI
Selected Poems 1954–94
Bilingual edition with translations by Peter France
978-0-946162-59-8

Gennady Aygi (1934–2006) is one of Russia's major modern poets, his free verse marking a radical new departure in Russian poetry. This is the most substantial presentation of his work published in the English-speaking world. 'Like Hopkins with English, Aygi makes the Russian language do things it has never done before.' – Edwin Morgan

PIERRE CORNEILLE
Horace
Translated by Alan Brownjohn
978-0-946162-57-4

This verse drama, its plot based on the legendary triple combat between two sets of brothers, the Horatii and the Curatii, to decide a war between Rome and Alba, lays bare the sinister nature of patriotism and has the power to challenge and disturb the modern reader with its unflinching reckoning of the personal cost of national glory. 'Corneille's rhyming alexandrines have been superbly translated into a flexible blank verse which captures the nuances of meaning.' – Maya Slater, *Times Literary Supplement*

HEINRICH HEINE
Deutschland: A Winter's Tale
Bilingual edition with translation by T. J. Reed
978-0-946162-58-1

A satirical travelogue on eve-of-1848 Germany which is engagingly modern – on customs union, women, food ... The wittiest work by Germany's wittiest poet. 'Reed succeeds beautifully in recreating the pointed, epigrammatic effect of the terse rhythm.' – Anita Bunyan, *Jewish Chronicle*

FERNANDO PESSOA
The Surprise of Being
Bilingual edition with translations by James Greene and Clara de Azevedo Mafra
978-0-946162-24-6

Twenty-five of the haunting poems written by Portugal's greatest modern poet in his own name, the most confounding of his voices. 'The translators have succeeded admirably in the task of rendering this most brilliant and complex of poets into inventive, readable English.' – *New Comparison*